Life's a Beach... in any Season

Warm up your winter—or any season—with this anthology of stories of springtime and summer love by members of the Ohio Valley Romance Writers of America. From heartwarming to mysterious, comical to suspenseful, these romantic tales show that there really is someone for everyone. Whether it happens today or a hundred years ago, from the Atlantic shore to the American West coast, there's something magical about the finding love when the warm breezes blow.

Love's a Beach

Stories of Summer Love

by members of the Ohio Valley Romance Writers of America

MYTHICAL PRESS ✴ DAYTON, OHIO

MYTHICAL PRESS * DAYTON, OHIO
www.mythicalpress.com

Love's a Beach
Edited by Lorie Langdon, Barbara Lohr, Michele Stegman, and
Mary Ulrich

"Tupelo Honey," "Rage and Compassion," "The Death of Harry," and
"I Wax, I Wane" © 2014 by Judy Carpenter
"The Ferris Wheel" and "The Wish" © 2014 by Stacy McKitrick
"Swizzle Stick" © 2014 by Sandy Pennington
"Titanic Love" © 2014 by Linda Chalk
"Sam, Kate, and the Lunch Lady's Secret" © 2014 by Daphne
Wedig-Griffis
"Time's Tempest: The Storm" © 2014 by Jennette Marie Powell
Cover design © 2014 Jennette Marie Powell
Photo © photocreo, used under license via www.fotolia.com

Table of Contents

Tupelo Honey

Ann Gregory

RAUL REYES LOOKED OUT THE SMALL WINDOW ABOVE his kitchen sink. He watched his neighbor hang clothes in her back yard, which abutted against his own back yard. "Saturday. Wash day." He looked up at the early April sun and noted the gentle breeze that billowed the clothes as she hung them. "They'll dry quickly."

She'd bought the pink stucco house behind his in Amelia, a suburb east of Cincinnati, several months earlier. Since then Raul hadn't spoken to her more than to say hello on those occasions when they met outside.

She was short, not quite five feet tall, and she struggled to keep her sheets from dragging the ground. Another neighbor had told him her name was Desdemona. It's a big name for a little woman.

The double lines on the clothesline posts sagged. She hung the sheets on both ends, then towels, and her clothes, then her underwear in the middle. The sheets and towels barely cleared the grass in the yard. He paused for a moment to smile at the brightly colored panties flanked by sturdy white bras. "She needs clothes line props."

Raul was a kind man. He had a soft spot in his heart for children, women, and animals. Any ill or hurting being, or even one in need, easily touched his heart. As Desdemona made her way to the door to her little house he made a decision. He would make her some clothes line props.

Though he'd retired from the landscaping company he'd owned for over thirty years, Raul still kept close ties to it. Knowing he would not be happy without something to occupy him, he had established his own landscape consulting company, with himself as the sole employee, which required only a few days of his time each month. The rest of his time was his to fill as he wished.

So the next morning after breakfast he drove to the nearest big box hardware store and purchased several lengths of narrow galvanized pipe and a couple of feet of heavy wire. Back home he set about making the clothes props.

He cut and bent the wire into loops and soldered them into one end of each pipe. Then he hammered the pipe ends around each wire to further keep it from coming out. Finally he pounded the bottoms of the pipes into wedges so they could be driven into the hard clay soil. When he finished, he checked each one. He nodded. "S'good."

Desdemona Smith was up late. She had lost her job after twenty-five years as a teller when a national chain bought the independent bank where she worked. Now she took night classes at the nearby university. She planned to earn an associates degree in early childhood education before her unemployment payments ran out. Tonight she was studying for a big test scheduled the next evening.

She wanted more tea and went to the kitchen. The bright moon shining through the small window over her sink gave sufficient illumination that she didn't need to turn on the overhead light. She filled her mug with the hot tea she kept on a warmer when movement in her neighbor's back yard caught her eye.

She smiled when she recognized her neighbor's loose white pajamas. Raul. He can't sleep again. He paced across his patio, turned, and paced back the other way. Her smile faded and she sighed.

She watched him flop into a lawn chair, sit for a minute, and then stand and resume pacing. "He needs warm milk, with tupelo honey."

Then she went to a cabinet and took out another mug and the jar of tupelo honey she kept there. She took milk from the fridge and heated it in a pot on the stove. When the milk was warm enough she poured it into the mug and added two tablespoons of the honey.

She looked out the window to make sure Raul was still there. He was sitting in the chair, so she took the two mugs and headed out the door. The screen door swung closed behind her with a screech, and she saw Raul's head rise and knew he watched her as she made her way across the yard.

When she got to her clothes line, she saw some strange posts stuck in the ground and holding up the line to a height several inches above her head. She counted four of them. "Where did those come from?" she asked aloud.

"I made them." Raul stood, but didn't approach her.

Desdemona spun around and almost dropped a mug. "Why?"

Raul felt a little uncomfortable. He had waited until dark to set out the line props, wanting them to be anonymous gifts. But when she stopped to look at them, for one wild moment, he wanted her to know he made them. Now, after his blurted confession, he regretted saying anything.

"Your towels were dragging the ground." To his own ears, his explanation sounded lame.

"Oh." She looked back at the poles, then looked at him. "Thank you."

The simple words pleased him. "You're welcome."

"This is for you." She held out a mug.

Raul took the mug from her hand and looked at the liquid inside. "What is it?"

Desdemona heard the note of suspicion in his voice and suppressed a smile. "It's warm milk with tupelo honey."

His eyebrows knitted together in confusion.

"When I can't sleep, I find warm milk and honey often

help me. Any honey will do, but I love tupelo honey."

He brought the mug to his nose and sniffed before taking a sip. "It's good!" His voice registered surprise.

"You might want to heat it up a bit."

"No, it's fine." He sipped again and motioned for her to sit in the woven lawn chair across from his on the patio, and then he sat.

She sipped from her own mug.

"Milk and honey for you, too?"

"No. This is hot tea. I was studying for a test when I saw you pacing, and on a whim decided to bring over the milk. I was ready for a short break, but I need to get back to the books." She sipped again, but didn't stand to leave.

"This is the best honey I've ever tasted. You said it's tupelo honey?"

"Yes. I order it online from Florida. It's collected from white tupelo trees. Pure tupelo honey won't crystallize and will keep for years.

"It's a little pricey, but so good I think it's worth it." She felt self-conscious when his eyes seemed to bore into her. She stood. "I've taken up enough of your time, and I need to get back to my books."

He drained his own mug, licked his lips, and handed the mug to her.

She started to walk away but stopped when he said, "Thank you."

She turned and smiled back. "You're welcome."

"I'm Raul," he called after her.

"I'm Desdemona," she called back.

Raul awoke the next morning and looked at the clock. When his eyes focused and he saw it was after ten, he was surprised. "I wonder if that milk and honey made me sleep better." He threw back the sheet, swung his legs to the side of the bed, and slipped his feet into the black Crocs he used for house shoes.

A few minutes later he sat at his kitchen table, a cup of coffee nearby and an egg sandwich in his left hand as he logged onto his laptop. He alternated between taking bites of the sandwich and sipping coffee as he began searching for a supplier of tupelo honey in Florida. He ordered a quart, paid with his credit card, and on impulse Googled Desdemona.

"Well, what do you know? She has a Facebook page."

As Facebook pages go, hers was rather simple. He found a picture of her, and a young man and young woman who resembled her, on her profile. Raul went to her "Photos" folder and saw two more pictures of her with the two. One picture showed her looking younger, with young children. In the other one she stood beside teenagers. It was clear from the age progressions the boy and girl were close to her.

Raul went back to her home page and found comments to "Mom" from both the young man, Colin, and young woman, Coco. "But no husband..."

As he paged through her posts he noticed she played

Farmville. Raul had started playing Farmville on those nights when he couldn't sleep. It was a safe alternative to late night TV and infomercials. He grinned and went to his own Facebook page and sent Desdemona an invite as a neighbor for Farmville.

Two days later Desdemona saw the Farmville invite from Raul. Surprised, she went to his home page on Facebook. His personal data said he had been employed at Berlew Landscaping Company for thirty years and had retired the previous year.

She clicked on his photos and saw several pictures. In the first one, he looked like he might have been maybe fifteen years younger. He was with a woman Desdemona assumed to be his wife, with two boys and two girls who looked to be between the ages of eight and fourteen. In the picture they were all smiling.

The next picture was of him with the four children, but the woman was missing. He and the children didn't look much older than in the first picture, but they all looked somber. The youngest girl looked like she might have been crying.

In the third picture Raul looked closer to his current age. He was surrounded by two young men and two young women. She could easily tell they were the same children from the first two pictures, but grown to adulthood. In this picture, the smiles were back.

"Doesn't look like he divorced her. Must have lost her to an accident, or illness."

She decided to accept his invitation, and soon they were helping each other build their farms.

The following Saturday, Desdemona began hanging her just-washed clothes on the line as usual. But now the new clothes props kept the sheets and towels from touching the ground. "Very good," she said aloud as she hung the last towel, and smiled.

She picked up her clothes basket and headed back into her house. In the kitchen she set down the basket and picked up the tea kettle and filled it with water at the sink. As it filled she looked out the window and saw Raul's back door open. He came out and flopped into a lawn chair. She could tell from his actions he was highly agitated.

She put the kettle on the stove and got out two mugs. When the kettle whistled, she made a mug of Darjeeling for herself and a mug of chamomile for him. She added a tablespoon of tupelo honey to each mug, took them both, and headed outside.

Raul saw Desdemona coming and wished he'd stayed inside. When he was aggravated, he preferred to be alone. But she held a mug in each hand and besides, she'd seen him, and it would be rude to go inside now. He sighed heavily and waited.

When she got to the patio she handed him a mug and sat in the chair opposite him. She said nothing.

He smelled the contents of the mug. Chamomile. He almost smiled. She thinks I need to be calmed down. He sipped the tea and recognized the tupelo honey. This time he allowed the smile to break across his face.

"Thanks."

She nodded but still didn't speak. Her eyes locked with his, and he started to squirm. But when he recognized both concern and kindness in her expression he relaxed and sighed again, a softer sigh.

"I used to work for a landscape company. I retired last year, but found I don't like being idle. So I offered to come back once a month to train employees on new products, methods, and equipment.

"The company requires their managers wear shirts with their logo on the left side pocket. For years the shirts were yellow, but recently they issued new blue shirts. At least mine were blue, until I washed them because they were stiff. Now they're kind of..." He hesitated. "Pink. I wasn't thinking. I threw a new red tee shirt in the washer with the work shirts.

"I have to give a seminar demonstrating new products Monday, and it's too late to order new shirts, even if I could overnight them, which I can't. So I have to choose between giving the seminar in an old yellow shirt, or a pink shirt."

He watched her face as he sipped, expecting her to

laugh, or at least smile. Instead she said in a quiet voice, "May I see them?"

He nodded and set his mug on the small table beside his chair. He went inside and returned shortly with four shirts. He held each one up in turn for her to examine.

Desdemona looked at the shirts. Pale pink streaks and spots were visible on each one, to greater and lesser degrees.

"I may be able to fix them. If I take them home, I could try, and return them tomorrow."

He looked at her for a moment before holding them out to her. "They're already ruined, so if it doesn't work, don't worry about it. Okay?"

She smiled. "Okay." She draped the shirts over her arm, drank the last of her tea, and stood.

He drank the last of his tea and handed her the mug. She smiled and returned to her house.

Raul watched her as she left, and realized he was watching her bottom more than anything else. He shook himself slightly and murmured, "Stop that!" He got up and went inside.

Later that afternoon Desdemona laid out the shirts on the back of her couch and stood back and looked at them. "Hmm. They're almost a denim blue. A light denim blue."

She needed to go to Walmart to pick up paper products. When she finished her regular shopping she made her way to the laundry aisle and the shelves of dye. She found a bottle of liquid denim blue and put it in the cart.

As she pulled out of the parking lot, she thought about Raul. He was not tall, but he was taller than she was. Maybe about five feet eight or nine inches tall. He had graying black hair, dark brown eyes, and his skin looked deepened from years of sun exposure. He was not a handsome man, nor was he unattractive. She supposed some people might describe him as plain. But she thought he had a pleasant face and a warm smile.

When she got home she put away the items she had bought, and then took the shirts and the dye to the laundry room. Before she started, she cut pieces of waterproof tape and covered the logos, front and back.

She pulled out the large plastic tub she'd used to dye items in the past. She rinsed it out and prepared the dye in the tub according to the directions on the bottle.

She knew timing was critical when dying clothes. If she left the shirts in too long, they would be too dark. If she didn't leave them in long enough, the pink wouldn't be covered. She stirred the shirts in the dye with a long steel fork, stopping periodically to lift one to look at the color.

Finally convinced the color was right, she removed the

shirts from the dye and rinsed them, first in the laundry tub and then in the washer. When she took them out of the washer she inspected each one. The pink was all gone, so she removed the tape from the logos and put the shirts in the dryer. Satisfied, she went upstairs and got ready for bed.

After breakfast the next morning Desdemona took the shirts out of the dryer and inspected them. Not a hint of pink, but they were slightly wrinkled. "I'll deal with the wrinkles after church." She went back upstairs and got ready.

Raul went through a burger drive-thru on his way home from church. At home he changed into more comfortable clothes before eating his burger and fries. He had popped the last fry into his mouth when he heard a knock on the kitchen door. He figured it was Desdemona and hurried to open the door.

She held out the four shirts on wood hangers. "I hope they're okay," she said. Her voice held a note of nervousness.

Raul took the shirts and inspected them. "I don't believe it. Not even a hint of pink! And the color is the exact shade but a little more..." He searched for a word.

"Vibrant?"

"Exactly. Vibrant. They're perfect."

Her expression went from apprehension to relief to pleasure.

"You kept me from the embarrassment of leading a seminar in an inappropriate shirt. Thank you."

She rewarded him with a broad smile. "It was nothing. Have a good day, and I hope your seminar goes well." She left, closing the door softly behind her.

As he hung the shirts in his closet, he smoothed them with a hand. "She pulled off a minor miracle. What a nice thing to do."

The next morning he dressed in khakis and one of his blue shirts. He packed an extra shirt in his briefcase, a habit he acquired years before when he attended board meetings instead of leading seminars. He knew from experience mishaps with coffee and other food items could result in a great deal of discomfort, especially when speaking in front of a group of people.

The seminar was scheduled in a large building behind a landscape storefront. There was a table set with coffee, juice, bagels, and Danish on one side of the room and the new landscaping equipment for Raul's demonstration up front. Rows of folding chairs occupied the middle. Raul made his way to the coffee.

As he poured himself a cup, another man came up beside him and mumbled something. Raul turned and said, "Excuse me?"

He instantly recognized John Fremont, the man assigned to help him with the demonstration. John wore one of the yellow shirts the managers used to wear.

"I said I'm sorry, Mr. Reyes. Our washer broke and my wife took our clothes to a laundry service. Everything came back but my new work shirts. I had no choice but to wear one of the old ones."

Raul smiled. "What size do you wear?"

"Large." John gave him a puzzled look.

"Come with me."

Raul took his extra shirt from his briefcase and handed it to John.

"You're kidding. You'd let me wear one of your special CEO shirts?"

"Retired CEO. And my shirts are nothing special."

"The color..."

Raul looked around at the other people in the room and realized his shirts were a tiny shade more, what word had Desdemona used? Vibrant. His shirts were more vibrant.

He looked back at John. "Maybe they're from a different dye batch."

The seminar was a success. Raul and John worked well together, and at the end of the day John returned his shirt, and Raul drove home, feeling good.

Desdemona sat, doing homework for one of her classes, when there was a knock on her back door. She looked out and saw Raul. When she opened the door he flashed a broad grin as he held out a small bag.

"I want to take you to dinner."

"Why?"

"Why? Does there have to be a why? Because I want to thank you for fixing the shirts."

"You already thanked me."

"But not properly. You didn't just save me, you saved another man."

"What are you talking about?"

"I'll tell you over dinner. "

"But I have homework to do. I have to do it tonight."

"Homework? How long will that take?" His eyebrows arched in surprise.

"At least another hour and a half. Maybe two."

Raul rubbed his chin. "You have to eat."

"I was going to heat leftovers."

"Leftovers?" He breathed deeply and then slowly let out his breath. "Do you like Indian food?"

"I love Indian food."

"I could pick up some Indian food and bring it in. You can spare an hour or so for carryout, can't you?"

The look on his face was so hopeful she didn't have the heart to deny him. "Yes. I can spare an hour, for carryout." And she smiled.

He turned to go but then said, "Oh. This is for you," He held out the bag. "I ordered tupelo honey."

She pulled a pint jar of the golden honey from the bag. "You didn't have to do that."

"Yeah, I did. When someone introduces me to something good, I like to return the favor. I got enough for both of us." Then he left.

She found the gesture touching, and she admitted to herself she appreciated the gift. On her tight budget, she might have decided against spending money on expensive honey.

Desdemona finished writing her essay for her early childhood development class on her laptop. She had just opened her book on recognizing and reporting suspected child abuse when there was another knock on the door. She opened it and Raul entered, a large shopping bag in his hand.

"We can eat in the living room. I have wooden folding tables. They're small, but it will be easier than trying to clear everything off the kitchen table."

"S'fine. Lead the way."

Raul set up the tables while she cleared the coffee table for the food. When he started setting out items she was stunned. "Did you buy everything on the menu?"

"We didn't discuss what you might like, so I got us a little of everything."

"I see."

While he opened the containers, Desdemona offered him sweet iced tea with his dinner.

He cocked his head slightly. "Sweetened with tupelo

honey, I hope?"

"Of course. What else?"

"Sounds great."

Within minutes they were spooning different items onto their plates, talking and laughing as they explored the contents of the containers. He told her about lending his extra shirt to John Fremont, and the comments from people over the "vibrancy" of their shirts.

She smiled and shook her head in wonder. "I only used liquid dye. No magic."

"Maybe no magic, but certainly a graceful end to a dilemma for John and me."

They smiled at each other, but Desdemona began to feel self-conscious. She looked away and took another bite of her chicken curry, and followed it with a bite of garlic naan.

"So what classes are you taking, and where?"

"I'm taking classes at the community college to become a day care director."

"Why a day care director, and why now?"

"I've been out of work for a while, on unemployment. I have a dear friend who owns a chain of day care centers and always needs a director for one center or another. She promised me a job as soon as I get my associate's degree and my director's license. The cost of tuition and books is eating into my savings, so I'm trying to finish as soon as possible. With summer classes I should be finished in August and get my license in the fall."

He smiled. "I admire your ambition and perseverance. A lot of people in your position wouldn't work so hard. Why didn't you take a student loan?"

"I don't want to spend the rest of my days paying off a loan, especially in this economy."

"Can I ask how old you are?"

"I'm forty-four, too young to retire, too old to go into deep debt. And how old are you?"

"Forty-nine."

"But you retired last year, after working thirty years. Wow. That means you started working at eighteen, and stayed at the same job the whole time." She didn't say it, but she wondered how he could afford to retire at such a young age.

As if reading her mind he said, "Besides teaching seminars, I do consultant work. After thirty years in the business, I'm pretty knowledgeable about landscaping, materials, and soil."

"Of course."

Desdemona took another bite of naan and looked at the clock on her mantle. After chewing and swallowing she said, "I really need to get back to my homework."

"Oh, yeah. I'm sorry. Which of these would you like to keep? There are more leftovers than I can eat alone."

They divided up the food and Desdemona walked him to the door. "Thanks for dinner. It was nice."

"It was nice." He smiled and left.

She locked the door after him and within moments she was immersed in her books again.

Back in his house, Raul poured himself a glass of Lambrusco wine. He thought back over the day, and was both gratified and strangely discontent.

He had always been of an analytical nature, which had been his greatest asset in building his company. He had learned he could use that approach to emotional problems as well as business problems.

He knew why he was gratified. The success of the seminar, the crisis of the shirts averted, the sharing of the extra shirt with John Fremont, and the sharing of the meal with Desdemona.

Desdemona.

He instantly realized his discontent centered round his neighbor and newfound friend, Desdemona Smith. But why?

He thought back to his wife, Ciri. She had passed away from cancer thirteen years ago, and he still ached for her. He had loved her from their first date, shortly after his nineteenth birthday. They married a year later, and he had never looked at another woman all their years together. For that matter, he hadn't looked at a woman since he had lost Ciri.

Until Desdemona.

Ciri could have been a poster child for a plain Latino woman. Dark brown eyes, black hair, light brown skin, a pleasant round face, and a figure that was neither thick nor thin.

But she had been beyond beautiful to him. It was her personality that had been most important to him. She laughed easily, she had a tender heart, she thought of others first, she was a great mother, and... she had loved him back.

No matter what success or failure he had experienced, she always encouraged him.

Remembering some of their shared moments during the tougher times in the earlier years, his stomach clenched and a gasp escaped his lips. A tear slipped from the corner of his eye, and he took a finger and wiped it away.

For the first time in many months he didn't fight the anguish of his loss. He let go and let the tears flow. He covered his face with his hands and cried, his shoulders shaking and his chest aching.

After a bit he stood and went to the bathroom, where he pulled off a length of toilet tissue and mopped his face and blew his nose.

Suddenly he had an image of Ciri in the darkest time of his struggle to make his business work. He had been so discouraged, and she had put her arms around his shoulders and said, "Raul, when I married you I didn't expect to be rich. But I wanted to be happy. I am happy. And if your business fails, it fails. We'll still be together, we'll still have the babies, and we'll make it. I know God will see us through. So quit fretting. It will work out the way it works out. And I'll still be happy, because I'll be with you."

He closed the lid of the commode and sat as tears flowed freely again.

It had been her words that had given him the strength and courage to make it. And as she predicted, it worked out. Only two years later he had made his first million dollars. And the only way it had affected Ciri was she started buying clothes at Sears instead of Goodwill.

Exhausted, he prepared for bed, expecting to be awake for a while. But as soon as he turned out the lights he fell asleep. It was a deep, dreamless sleep.

When Raul left, Desdemona had no problem getting back to her homework. But as soon as she closed the last book and her laptop and put everything into her messenger bag, she started thinking about her neighbor.

She felt uneasy. Her marriage had ended in divorce after ten years when Carl had come in and announced he no longer loved her and left. It didn't take long for her to discover he had been in an affair with a woman in his office for over a year. Carl had made no attempt to see her or the children again.

Things had been hard, but they had made it. Now Colin and Coco had both graduated from college and were making their way in their chosen careers. Until she lost her job at the bank, she'd been having the first financial freedom she'd ever enjoyed in her life. And then she had met Winston.

Winston had been so nice at first. He wined and dined her, and made himself comfortable around her and her friends and family. But slowly, over the months he became more demanding, more controlling, and more... needy. The need usually centered around money.

The wakeup call for her came when he became belligerent, even threatening, when she purchased a new pair of pumps for church. He demanded she take them back at once. When she refused, his tactic changed.

He fell onto a chair and burst out in tears. Through sniffs and sobs he admitted he had been gambling, and begged her for ten thousand dollars, or his bookie would "break both his kneecaps." She had almost fallen for it.

But when she went into the bank to get the money the teller said, "I was surprised to hear you remarried. When your new husband came in to cash a check on your account yesterday, we had to deny him. You'll need to have him come in with you to fill out paper work to add him to your account."

Shocked, Desdemona pulled the ten thousand dollar draft back and tore it into pieces. "I suggest you call the police. I didn't marry anyone."

With the help of a good lawyer, Winston had managed to stay out of jail, but at least he was out of her life, and her money was intact. But the experience made her realize she didn't want or need another man in her life.

Her thoughts returned to Raul, and she shivered. He wasn't drop-dead gorgeous, but he was certainly handsome to her. She liked it when he smiled, when he laughed, and she wondered what it would be like to kiss him.

She hated to admit it, but she liked him. A lot. More than Winston, and even a lot more than she had ever liked Carl. But that made him a distraction, and she didn't need any distractions. Not now.

She shook her head. "I'm staying away from Raul Reyes from now on!" Her words echoed against the kitchen walls.

The first thought Raul had when he awoke the next morning was of Desdemona, not Ciri. He thought of her expressive blue eyes. He remembered the vulnerability he saw in them when she waited for him to pass judgment on his shirts. It was easy to read her thoughts just by looking into her eyes.

He thought of the way she tucked her dark hair behind her ear to move it out of her eyes. How she looked when she laughed. The way her lips moved when she chewed, when she spoke. He thought of her bottom when she walked away...

He thought of Ciri, and he sat straight up in bed and shouted, "Stop that!"

He decided he needed to avoid Desdemona Smith.

Raul and Desdemona didn't interact with each other at all for over two weeks. Saturday was wash day. For the past two Saturdays she had used the dryer for her clothes. But today the May sun was shining, the breeze was perfect, and she decided to hang her wash outside.

She had a full basket and her pins, but she peeked out the door before leaving the kitchen. Raul wasn't in sight, so she hurried outside. She hung her clothes and then rushed back inside, leaving her basket behind.

Raul looked out his window and saw her hanging clothes. He backed away, in case she might glance his way and see him. He was aware of a feeling of regret, of... loss? He sighed heavily and poured himself a glass of cold tea, sweetened with tupelo honey. It wasn't very satisfying.

When Desdemona got back inside, she heard an odd sound—the sound of rushing water. She followed it to her wash room and found water gushing from a hole in the wall where a pipe had obviously burst. Water already puddled an inch thick on the floor.

In a panic, she started to run out back and shout for Raul, but caught herself.

Then she remembered the water shut-off valve. She ran outside and found the valve and quickly turned it. She ran back inside, checked to make sure the water had stopped, and then started looking up plumbers. She found one willing to come out on a Saturday. After she gave him directions she hung up and began cleaning up the mess.

The rest of her day was taken up with the water situation. When the plumber left she looked at the giant hole in the wall he'd had to cut to fix the pipe. She would have to have someone come in and repair the drywall and baseboard.

She filled a spray bottle full of bleach and soaked everything where the water had stood. After opening the window, she set up the two fans she owned to try to dry out the room. She didn't need a toxic fungus on top of everything else.

She looked at the clock. It was after eight, and she was exhausted. She made a sandwich which she ate hastily and then brushed her teeth and got ready for bed.

A clap of thunder woke her. She started to nestle further under the covers when she remembered. "My clothes! They'll be ruined!"

She jumped out of bed and slipped into her old canvas shoes and ran to the kitchen. She threw open the door and ran outside to the clothes line.

Raul had watched all afternoon for Desdemona to get her clothes, but she never showed. Eventually he realized she must have forgotten them.

That night was one of those nights when he couldn't sleep. He wanted to sit on the patio, but was afraid she might remember her clothes and he wouldn't be able to get inside without speaking to her.

The first couple of claps of thunder didn't get his attention, but a particularly loud one broke through. "Her clothes! They'll be ruined!" He jumped up and ran outside.

When Desdemona got to the clothes line, she saw Raul already standing there, taking off pins and tossing clothes into the basket. He was drenched, his hair glued to his head. Rain ran down his face and dripped to mix with the water already pooling on the ground.

When he saw her he stopped. "You forgot your clothes. It's raining."

"I... I... I had a plumbing problem. A pipe burst. There was water all over..."

He looked at her, and she became self-conscious again. She looked down, which was a mistake. His white cotton pajamas were plastered to his body, and she saw the complete outline of his form. She gasped and quickly looked up again.

She obviously doesn't realize her pajamas are soaked, and I can see right through them. If he hadn't been paralyzed with a dozen different emotions, he might have realized the same thing about himself.

Abruptly he took the pins and the towel he held and threw them into the basket. In seconds he closed the gap between them and wrapped his arms around her. He picked her up and looked into her face. The water dripped from both their noses, the thunder crashed over their heads.

"I've missed you. Really missed you," he said.

"I've missed you, too. Really missed you."

He slowly bent his head and found her lips with his and

kissed her eagerly. Wonder of wonders, she returned the kiss as eagerly.

When their lips parted, they looked at each other for a long moment before he said, "It's crazy standing here in the rain like this. Let's finish and get inside before we both end up with pneumonia."

She nodded. They got the rest of the clothes down and he grabbed the basket and they headed for her house.

Inside the kitchen he set down the basket and grabbed her and kissed her again. He discovered this kiss was every bit as wonderful as the first one.

This time when they broke away he said, "You're shivering, and I'm freezing. Can I take you to lunch after church tomorrow?"

She simply nodded, and he kissed her again, on the nose, and left.

Their lunch the next day was the first of many dates. Over the next three months Raul and Desdemona spent a lot of time together, and their relationship deepened. They were both surprised, and gratified, to find such a strong bond after giving up on romance.

One evening in late August Raul and Desdemona sat at a table on the patio of a restaurant in New Richmond. They were only a few yards from the Ohio River bank and they could hear the gentle lapping of the water against the rocks on the bank. They were celebrating Desdemona's graduation and her associates degree. The only thing left was to get her day care director's license.

Raul took a sip of water and swallowed. "Desdemona?"

"Yes?"

"I think we should get married."

"You do?" She cocked her head to the side.

"Yes. You see, I love you."

It was her turn to sip water and swallow. "You do?"

"Yes. And I think you love me. Do you?"

"Yes."

"Then we should get married." He pulled a ring box from his coat pocket and set it before her.

Her mouth turned down in a frown, but her eyes twinkled. "You want to marry me because soon I'll be making the big bucks, at the day care center."

He smiled and chewed his lower lip before saying, "Are you going to open it?" He nodded at the box.

She wiped her lips with her napkin, took the box, and lifted the lid. She was stunned and silent for a moment. Then she looked at him through narrow eyes, "Is this real?"

"It is. Real white gold. Real sapphires. Real diamonds."

She closed the box with a snap and pushed it toward him. "Take it back and get something more sensible. I'm not letting you go into that kind of debt at your age."

He threw back his head and laughed until big tears rolled down his cheeks. It wasn't until he recognized the pain and anger in her eyes that he managed to control himself and stopped laughing.

"Sorry. But you are so precious."

She glared at him, and he looked away. "I was eighteen when I started working for Berlew Landscaping. I loved it from day one.

"I was twenty when I married Ciri. When I was twenty-two Mr. Berlew took me aside and said he wanted to sell the company and retire. He offered it to me, and even helped me find financing. Ciri and I were ecstatic.

"The first couple of years were rough, but we learned, and became profitable. A couple of years later I opened a satellite company in another town. Soon I opened a third, a fourth... Eventually I had twenty."

He was silent for a moment. "Then I lost Ciri."

His knew his face and voice reflected the sadness he felt, and she touched his hand to comfort him. He closed his eyes, but he smiled and reopened them.

"We had just put the company up for sales of public shares, and I was CEO. But without someone to share it with, it was an empty victory. So last year I retired, but I still own the majority of shares."

"But, why do you live in that tiny house?"

He smiled again. "It was the first house Ciri and I bought. I never sold it. When the children all grew up and moved out I rattled around by myself in our big house, and I was miserable. So I sold it and moved back to what felt to me like home."

He took the ring from the box and reached for her left

hand and slipped it on her finger. "There is no loan. I paid cash."

She held out her hand and looked at it. The ring sparkled in the sunlight. "I'm still not convinced you're not just after my money."

"Well, I was hoping you'd pay for dinner..."

She covered her mouth with her hand and stifled a laugh, but he laughed out loud.

He stood and came around and bent down and kissed her. It was a long, lingering, satisfying kiss. When he broke away he went back and sat down.

"When Ciri died, my life all but ended. I thought I'd never be able to love any woman again. And then you showed up with a mug of warm milk and tupelo honey, and gave me back everything I'd lost. I love you, Desdemona."

"I love you too, Raul."

The Ferris Wheel
Stacy McKitrick

JUST LOOKING UP AT THE MONSTROSITY CAUSED VIOLET'S stomach to churn, but she couldn't look away. Did it sway? No, wait. That was her. She had hoped the Ferris wheel looked smaller in daylight. She couldn't have been more wrong.

"What did I ever do to you?" She finally tore her eyes away and looked at Crystal. "I'll ride any other ride here. Why this one?"

"You sound like you're afraid of a stupid ride."

"Who, me? Nah." Make that terrified. Somehow she had to get out of this without letting Crystal know what a wimp she had as a friend. "It's just not one of my favorites. All it does is go 'round and 'round. Kind of boring, don't you think?"

"Then it's not a problem, right? Besides, I have a secret weapon. Something not so boring."

"What kind of secret weapon? What are you up to?"

Crystal looked over Violet's shoulder and frowned. "Well?"

Violet turned to see who Crystal was questioning. Oh, her boyfriend, Brandon. Was he her secret weapon? Brandon was nice and all, but belonged to Crystal.

"Hey Babe," Brandon said. "He's coming." He placed his arm around Crystal's waist before giving her a kiss on her temple. Violet smiled at his personal display of affection.

There wasn't anyone in her life like that.

"Who's coming?" Violet asked.

Crystal grinned like she had something up her sleeve. "Nick," she said.

The mention of his name caused Violet's chest to constrict. "Nick? As in Nick Roberts?"

"You called?"

Violet turned at the sound of his voice. His nice, deep, sexy sounding voice. What was he doing here? The last time she saw him, she had made a fool of herself by asking him out. And why would she think he'd ever want to go out with her? It wasn't like she was shapely like Crystal. Unless you call straight a shape. Her hair had no curl, no bounce, and it certainly wasn't blonde like most of the women that fawned over him. Those other women also didn't wear glasses. Violet was blind without hers. Still, they'd been friends for nearly a year and she thought he liked her, so she risked asking him out. Even though his rejection was sort of expected, it still hurt. That had been two months ago; she hadn't seen him since.

And now he was standing there, not two feet away, looking as hunky as ever. His t-shirt fit him like a second skin, accentuating the muscular body he owned. She knew he'd been working out, just not how much. The sight caused a lump to form in her throat.

He gazed at her and she was lost in his brown eyes.

"Hey, Violet. Thanks for meeting me here."

Violet snapped her head toward Crystal. "Meeting?"

she mouthed.

"Why don't we go stand in line and we can talk about it there?" Crystal said.

Violet's legs refused to move. Riding the ride was one thing. Riding beside Nick quite another. "I'll just wait in the beer garden." Yeah, a drink would do her good. "You all go on without me."

"Please, don't go," Nick said as he took her arm and slipped it through his.

What was with his plea? She wasn't the one who stopped calling. She wasn't the one who ended the friendship.

Her mind refused to budge, but once he touched her, once those strong hands took her arm, her body didn't care. It just followed right along with the rest of the gang; her mind be damned.

"You're so tense. Are you afraid of the ride?" Nick asked.

"No, of course not." She followed it with a chuckle. Too bad it sounded weak. No way would she admit her fear to him, though. He already thought she was a foolish-love-sick girl, why add scared-of-a-kiddie-ride to the list?

What the heck was Crystal up to anyway? Why Nick? Why the Ferris wheel? Could a person die of fear? Of mortification? God, she hoped not.

The four of them reached the back of the line and fell in place. Standing in line? Easy. Moving in line? Possible. Getting on that ride? Oh shit. Would she make a scene?

Maybe for once she could be brave and just ride the ride. What's the worst that could happen? Falling? Death? If she was going to die, she had a right to know why.

Violet leaned into Crystal and whispered into her ear. "Why did you invite Nick? Have I done something wrong? If so, I'm sorry. I'll clean the apartment; I'll do your laundry. Just don't punish me like this."

Nick laughed. Crap. He heard her?

"It's not Crystal's fault," he said. "I asked her to bring you."

Violet spun around. "You did? But—"

"And my job is done," Crystal said. "See you in a little while." She grabbed Brandon's arm and dragged him off as he smiled and waved goodbye.

Violet stared at Crystal's retreating body. The traitor. How could she? She knew what Nick meant to her. She knew how he broke her heart.

The line was moving much too fast. Violet's heart started skipping beats. Sweat trickled down between her breasts. How was she going to get out of this without looking like a total psycho?

Nick stood behind her and placed his hands on her shoulders. She jumped. "Relax, Violet. I'm not gonna bite. Nothing bad will happen."

He gently massaged her shoulders. Now she didn't know if she was jumpy because of the ride or because of his touch. Every muscle in her body clenched. She closed her eyes, trying to relax, while he continued to massage and propel her forward.

"Next."

Her eyes flew open. The attendant was standing there

holding the bar so they could slide onto the seat. The next thing she knew, she was sitting beside Nick. Her heart stopped and she held her breath. What was she doing? "I have to get off."

"You're not going anywhere. We need to—"

"I'm afraid of the ride!" There, she said it. Mortification complete.

"Then give me these." Nick gently removed her glasses.

"Hey!" She reached out for them, but once they were off her eyes everything became blurry. "I can't see without them."

"I know. You can't be afraid of something you can't see. Just pretend we're sitting on a porch swing. Close your eyes if it'll make it better."

She could almost buy into that, until the swing started to move. They were apparently the last ones to embark as the ride didn't stop to let any more passengers on. She was fine as the swing rose, but once it started downward, her throat met her stomach.

"Oh God." She reached out to grab the bar and found his hands instead. He didn't move them so she concentrated on the warmth of his skin instead of the movement of the ride.

"I want to apologize, Violet."

"I might forgive you if I live through this. Why don't we wait and see?"

Nick chuckled. "Not about the ride. About how I acted when you asked me out."

Words escaped her. She did not want to have this conversation.

"You kind of shocked me," he continued. "I didn't think you were interested in me that way."

How could anyone not be interested in him that way? He was the sweetest person she knew and looked even better. Didn't he know that?

"It wasn't until after you left that I started thinking about you. I missed your jokes. I missed the little digs you gave me whenever I said something inappropriate. I missed you."

Did she hear him right? He missed her? His fingers touched her chin and he turned her face to him.

"Violet." His face was close to hers, his breath minty. "I want to kiss you."

She lamely nodded. Was this really happening? He didn't like her. Did he? His lips were soft and warm and she melted into him. A fire burned deep inside her and she brought her hand up to the back of his head just as the Ferris wheel came to a jarring halt.

She grabbed onto the first thing within reach—his hair. "What's happening?"

He muttered a curse and gently uncurled her fingers from his hair. "It's okay, Violet. You can let go. Nothing's happening. They're starting to let people off."

She pulled her hand away. "I'm sorry. It's just that I can't see."

"Then maybe you should put these back on." When she realized he was putting her glasses on her face, she finished the process. Nick came back into focus, looking as handsome as ever and grinning from ear to ear.

"Now, don't you feel better?"

The ride moved to the next position and jerked to another stop. Is that why he kissed her? To keep her from embarrassing him? Oh God, could this day get any worse? She pulled back and scooted away, keeping her eyes down.

"Violet, what's the matter?" He slid closer to her.

Why was he tormenting her? What had she ever done to him but like him? "You tricked me?" she murmured.

His arm went around her shoulders. She wanted to die. Wasn't it enough she made a fool of herself before? Now he only rubbed it into her face. Her vision became blurry and this time it wasn't from the lack of her glasses.

"I'm sorry if it seems that way. I really didn't know you were afraid of the ride when I asked Crystal to arrange the meet. I figured it was an excuse to get away. I just wanted to get you alone somewhere where you couldn't run from me."

He wasn't making any sense. "Why would I run from you?" For two months she dreamed he'd make contact of some sort. For two months she lived in disappointment.

"Because you never returned my calls," he said.

No way. Now she knew he was lying. "You never called. I can prove it." She fished her phone out of her pocket and opened it up. After pushing several buttons, she lifted the phone and showed him her call list. "See, no calls from you."

He looked at the phone for a moment and then his eyebrows rose. "Violet, my number is there. You just don't have my name assigned to it."

"What?" On the display were the calls she had been getting from "Caller Unknown". She looked in her address book and found his name, but the last two numbers had been transposed. How the hell had she done that?

"So, you were hoping I would call?" he asked. "You don't hate me?"

God no, she could never hate him. She was afraid she'd screwed up their friendship. She smiled when it hit her: he likes me.

When she started to tell him, she scanned the horizon. Oh, God, the ground was so far away. She gripped the hand rail and started to hyperventilate. Nick sprang into action and claimed her mouth with his. She could kiss him forever; she was in heaven. When she heard someone cough, she opened her eyes. The attendant was waiting for them to get off.

How could she ever hate the Ferris wheel if it gave her Nick?

Violet batted her eyes at Nick. "Want to ride it again?"

Swizzle Stick
SANDY PENNINGTON

HER NAME WAS GAY, AND SHE WAS ANYTHING *BUT*.

Her job was in the kitchen, scrubbing dishes, making mugs sparkle and shine. But that idiot, Doreen, blew off work again, leaving the bar shorthanded. Anxiety gripped her. Reluctantly, she pinned on her name tag. It read, 'I'm Gay'. With a name like hers, Gay knew she was in for a fun time.

This was so not what she wanted. She reached for an apron, dragging her feet. When the place was crazy with people, she happily prepped food right beside Jake, the master sandwich maker. A few people she could handle. But dealing with the demands and attentions of strangers? That made her sick inside.

"Hey! You coming out here anytime soon?" bellowed Topeka, the waitress with the stunning good looks.

"Yeah, yeah, I'm almost ready!" she yelled back.

Gay turned her back from the door. A quick pat down assured her that the necessary items were in place: phone, credit cards, cash. All shoved into her ultra-cushy bra. Her multi-pocket cargo pants carried a miniature flashlight, Swiss Army knife, and her key to freedom, a 1999 Toyota. Clothing, bottled water, dried fruit, and her precious sticks were in the beat up knapsack in the trunk of the car.

Gay pulled her shirt out from her waistband. She opted

for the shapeless, bulky look when dealing with the bar people. The alcohol huggers. The obnoxious ass patters. She had her fill of pat downs, thank you very much.

"God," she whispered, "If only Uncle Simon hadn't died..." If only she hadn't been implicated. Framed. And forced to do time.

If only.

Thoughts of the past triggered heat spikes that gushed through every pore of her body. Her brain shut down as moisture beaded on her forehead. Unsteady, she reached for the nearest counter.

Oh, this was just great! she fumed to herself. She hadn't even dealt with her first customer yet, and already she was breaking out into a sweat. If she didn't calm down, the raised welts would follow. On top of everything else, she didn't need to look like a flaming strawberry tonight.

"You ok, kid?" asked Jake. He knew she hated to go out and mix with folks.

"I'll be alright in a second." Her hands fanned her face, making a breeze. Stop it, she told herself. Anger and shame, her twin demons, warred back and forth. Then she remembered to count. Three, six, nine, twelve, fifteen, and on.

And on.

Seconds passed. Heat faded. It was time for her to put her mean face on.

Hennesey watched the young woman sprint past his table. Again. His fingers had begun tapping out an endless tattoo. He wasn't used to waiting. Or being ignored. Bummer for him, finding out what a bitch it was when you couldn't flash your badge around and seize everyone's attention.

"Miss?" he tried once more, waving his mug in the air. Another "no go" as far as catching her eye. "Hey!" he finally shouted, causing everyone but his server to turn around and stare at him. Oh, that was real mature, he chided himself. Being a U.S. Marshal had its privileges no doubt, but when said officer was out on medical leave, with no case churning his gut? Evidently, not so much, thought Hennesey, lowering his eyes.

Maybe playing this particular version of 'Pin The Tail on the GPS Donkey' wasn't such a good idea. He left town against medical advice, the ambulatory center's protest still burning his ears. He'd driven for hours, wanting to escape, his only companions his antibiotic pills and haphazard bird droppings he collected along the way. He found himself headed for Delaware, parts unknown. He pulled over and searched out his location.

'Hauntingly beautiful Devil's Tooth Cove' caught his eye. 'Off Route One that hugs the Atlantic coastline' was the map's promise. A beach. Ocean. Open sky. He followed the highway arrow blindly to this off-the-beaten path spot. What the map didn't say was how difficult it would be for an ordinary guy to get some food and drink at Mr. Woo's Watering Hole.

A hard slap on the table jarred him out of his pitiful thoughts. A bowl of pretzel nuggets had miraculously appeared.

"And what the hell can I get you tonight?" asked the woman he'd been waiting for. "I saw you waving at me earlier—I just couldn't come over right away."

Hennesey was shocked at her less than gracious greeting. He read her name tag—it said 'Gay.' But she didn't act happy, or look the least bit sorry for making him wait. Though disturbed by her entrance, he was even more disturbed with himself. He hadn't seen her approaching at all. He was distracted, lost in reverie. How stupid, and worse, how dangerous for someone like him. He shifted in his seat. Being classified as unfit for duty infuriated him. Now he wondered if the talking heads in the white lab coats weren't right after all.

Hen cleared his throat. "You got any menus around here? I'm starving."

He leaned back in his chair and sized her up. First impressions were everything to him. A quick glance over showed she was in her late twenties, about 5'5", with an oval face that could have been pretty. Mid-length jet black hair and darker eyes, he noted, with clothes that hung on her like a sack. No change in facial expression. Hunched shoulders. Not a whole lot of eye contact. There wasn't a bit of gloss or shine about her. But he needed to eat, he reminded himself. It was almost time to take his mega pills.

"We don't need menus at Mr. Woo's," said Ms. Unfriendly.

"We have simple food, and of course, no fries."

Hen straightened up at her words, wincing at the cracking sound his back made. Surely he hadn't heard correctly.

Loud irate grumbling sounds came from his stomach while his brain processed this latest setback. A snack shack practically on a beach, and it didn't serve fries?

"Really? No fries?" Hen swallowed his disappointment. "Well, how about a cheese burger? Can you do a double burger with tomatoes, lettuce—" But the woman was already shaking her head 'No' to him.

Hennesey couldn't believe it. This was beyond what was reasonable. "Is this a restaurant or not?" he demanded. He reached out and grabbed her arm. Didn't she understand that he was tired and hungry and—

"Let. Go. Of. My. Arm," she said in a pointed measured tone. "Now!"

Damn if the woman didn't hiss at him like a snake. Hennesey dropped said body part like he'd been bit by a rattler, stunned at his own behavior. What was he thinking, grabbing her arm like that? Getting rough to make a point was never his style. At least, not when he was trying to order food, he reasoned.

He gritted his teeth, refusing to apologize. "I give up. No fries. No menus. Just what the hell is there to eat around here?"

The faintest of smirks touched her mouth before she spoke. "Sandwiches," she began. "Ham and cheese. Or just ham, or, just cheese." Her eyebrows lifted a fraction. "We sell them by the inch. And of course, there is the 'Sea Witch' special. Crab cakes with cukes, carrots and celery. Fresh cut, with au jus of lime dipping sauce."

Hennesey's jaw dropped. It was outrageous, and the most he'd heard out of her mouth yet. "That's it?" His temper was rising as was the familiar ache on his left side. "Are you kidding me? How about chicken wings?"

The waitress wore a serious expression, her forehead creased with a frown. The smooth black cap of her hair curved under her chin, hugging both sides of her face. Once more her head swayed from side to side in a negative motion.

It was beyond Hennesey to break eye contact her. "Potato skins with chili?" he pleaded, absently placing his left hand under his jacket and rubbing his side.

"Oh, no, mister," explained Ms. Unsympathetic. "Mr. Woo does not deep fry or heat anything, 'cause of fire, ya know? Except for the crab cakes. They go in the oven, timed perfectly, and come out hot and moist." She took a deep breath. "Then there is our famous coffee too. Folks really seem to like Devil's Cove fresh ground."

"Really?" Hen was starting to feel a bit lightheaded. Maybe he should switch from beer to something with caffeine in it. "What's so special about your coffee?" Surely, he thought, that was a safe question to ask.

"Well. It's just...Hot. Coffee." She spoke slowly, and emphasized each word, like he was an idiot who could not grasp plain English.

Hennesey gave his head a shake and took stock of his

surroundings. Country music twanged in the background. Soft blue and green lights twinkled in the fish nets hanging on the wall. Mermaids in all shapes and sizes dangled from the ceiling. People chatted as digital televisions streamed every sport imaginable.

For the space of a second, his vision narrowed. It seemed to be just the two of them, a man and a woman caught up in a bar scene, one being repeated across bars everywhere throughout the universe. So why, he wondered, was it so hard for him to get something to eat in this podunk joint?

"Hey!" she demanded. "I haven't got all day! Do you want something or not?"

Hennesey was floored. Her voice jarred him back to cold hard reality. How in hell did this chick even keep her job? His hunger raged. The need for food prevailed. He cleared his throat, as if he had an important announcement to make.

"I will take a cheese sandwich on wheat..." But, to his chagrin, Ms. Uncooperative was shaking her head 'No' again! "What, now?" he asked. "Let me guess. No wheat bread, right?"

"Yeah," she replied, "No wheat. No white either. Just plain Hawaiian. Yours will be right up!"

Before he could even ask if he could have a lousy pickle, she had turned on her heel and was gone. Five minutes later, Hennesey was left with a dry as dust throat, and a still empty mug. 'Sawdust for food and spit for drink,' wailed his stomach to his brain. Maybe he should get up and get his own damn drink. He started to lift his tired butt to do just that when an irritating voice floated over to him.

"Touch me again and I swear I will kick your ass right on outta here!" His eyes zeroed in on the not-so-gay waitress, who stared pointedly at the beefy hand laying on her arm. "Now do you want this sandwich or not?" asked Ms. Pissed Off.

Hennesey fell back into his chair, fascinated by the unfolding situation a few feet away. He found himself leaning forward, wanting to catch more of their byplay. Damn if he wasn't gawking—just like those despised people who ringed crime scenes.

He scratched at the stubble that shadowed his face. Hell, he thought, if this was entertainment, he definitely needed to get out more. Yet, he couldn't take his eyes off of her.

"Aw, come on!" shot back the irate customer. "You call this pitiful thing a sandwich? For five bucks, lady, I could get a foot-long somewhere else!"

Hennesey saw the man slowly release the arm in question, one finger at a time. He noted the guy had a crew cut and looked big and wide, like he was used to tackling people to make a point. For a moment, the customer stilled his hand above the offending food.

Hen saw the man's fingers arch, and form an "O." Uh-oh, he thought.

A sudden flick of the man's middle finger sent the bread topper airborne—soaring right across the table before finally hitting the floor. Hoots of laughter, hands slapping high fives, and rounds of "Woot! Woot!" circled the immediate area.

Hunger clawed at Hennessey's insides like a tiger's paw. He cursed the idiots in front of him, adults hell-bent on playing with their food. But most of all, he cursed the fact he couldn't reach the bread, dammit.

"Let me remind you, sir," he heard Ms. Attitude counter in a clear no-nonsense voice, "You ordered the two finger slice option." Her chin was up, her shoulders squared. She was ready to do battle.

Hen sat up a little straighter so he wouldn't miss a thing.

"These sandwiches are made to be light—more like an appetizer," she continued. "If you had bothered to listen to me the first time, you could have ordered the four or sixth width slice." The "So, there!" was unspoken, but it hung in the air between them.

Hen was starving but this was better than cable! He didn't have long to wait for the punch line.

"Oh, honey," said the customer in a false sympathetic voice, "I can do soooo much better than two fingers," he purred.

There was a moment of dead silence, then chuckles erupted. Back slapping was soon followed by cries of "Bro! You the man!"

Hennesey had to smother a laugh, still not able to look away from the two perpetrators. Now the issue of sexual harassment had been raised. He should know, he attended class after class on the subject. Sure, the guy had acted like a total jerk, but, when he thought of the rudeness that female dished out....

A second passed. Then Ms. Prickly Pear stepped back, a deadpan expression on her face. "I will be right back with your bill," she said carefully. Then she tilted her head a bit and added, "You arrogant asshole."

"Hey! Wait just a minute!" the man hollered, but, too late—the waitress turned and walked away. "I demand to see the manager right now!" he roared, scraping back his chair, all but leaping out of his seat.

Well, thought Hennesey. What an exit! He looked around, seeing people laughing. Drinking. Eating. Something he dearly wanted to do. He spied his waitress stomp through some doors by the bar, the nasty man hot on her tail. He sighed, sure his food order was totally forgotten by now.

Slowly, he got up, his left side stinging a bit more. It was late, and the place was getting louder. Feeling a bit shaky, he picked his way towards the bar, hoping someone would take pity, and let him order carry out.

Hen sat in his car shoving mouthfuls of food into his craw like there was no tomorrow. Damn, it was good! So far he demolished two, four inch cheese sandwiches, and was working on his third crab cake. Sweet-fiery lime sauce dripped from his fingers onto his jeans, but, he could have cared less. After licking his fingers clean—that damn Mr.

Woo had a good thing going, he decided—he fished around for his horse pills.

A sudden burst of music broke the peace, signaling activity by the front door. He saw the offensive loud mouth being strong armed by a bouncer. It figures, he thought. That poor slob gets the shaft while Ms. Cranky gets to keep her job. Thank God it wasn't his problem.

He grabbed his Coke with extra ice and popped three pills into his mouth. Taking a big swallow, he shook out three more. Down they went. Sated and stuffed to the gills, he adjusted his leather seat and leaned back. The press of a button opened the sun roof to ocean fresh air and the incredible night sky. He wondered how far away the beach was. Telling himself he just needed a minute before heading out again, he let the peaceful moment wash over him.

"Don't come near me!"

Hennesey blinked. That annoying voice again. It was so close. So real. Had he dreamt it?

He jerked upright. What the hell? Had he actually fallen asleep in the car? He felt heavy. Lethargic. And careless. Things a marshal should never feel when on his own. He slapped his hand against the steering wheel furious with himself all over again. His stomach churned a protest too. The rich food and high powered antibiotics were not settling well. He willed the queasiness away just as a familiar pain made its presence felt.

Hennesey's hand crept to his left side. Intense heat came through his clothing. Who knew that a simple stab wound would take so long to heal? He needed to find lodging and change his bandage: the soap, water and Neosporin regimen an absolute priority for him. It was eleven p.m. and he still had to drive back to the interstate. Key in hand, he reached for the ignition.

"Stay-away-from-my-car!"

The words—a female's words—slammed into him, catching him unawares. He recognized fear and apprehension when he heard it. Someone was in trouble and he had a gut feeling he knew who it was. The waitress from hell. Should he go for help? Intervene? He was such a sucker for the female in distress thing. He let out deep sigh, and pushed down on the door handle. Guess he wasn't leaving Mr. Woo's just yet.

"Think you're pretty smart, don't you? Making me look stupid in front of my friends like that!"

Hennesey focused, and followed the new voice, picking his way carefully through gravel and grass. He headed towards the rear of the restaurant where it was darker. He could see a stairway to the left side of the building with a solitary bulb shining above a door. Much good that was, he noticed, observing how a clump of trees that shaded during the day, absorbed every bit of light at night.

"Look, mister, go home! It's over!"

Hennesey stumbled upon them, not liking what he saw. It was the Incredible Bulk and The Mouth, going at it again.

The man had a white box in one hand and something else in the other. The woman was edging around the side of a car in little steps. He could see she was agitated, pacing back and forth, back and forth. She had a clear path to the restaurant's rear door. Why the hell wouldn't she take it?

"Go home," she said again. "No one wants any trouble here, OK?"

"Trouble? Oh, you've got trouble aplenty, girlie," the man threatened. With that he threw the box at her.

One moment, Hennessey saw flying round things that thudded harmlessly to the ground. A light fishy smell touched the air.

Crab cakes to go? he wondered. The man let loose his other hand, sending a rock straight for the car's windshield.

"Hey!" the woman wailed, the sound of glass shattering the night. "Not my car!" she cried, hurrying to the front of it to survey the damage. "What the hell is the matter with you? Look what you've done!"

"That's nothing compared to what I'm going to do to you!" was the ugly response. The big guy moved closer.

Well, crap, thought Hennesey. He had seen and heard enough. Verbal threats. Physical menacing. Destruction of personal property, were the tally of charges so far. What else was the goon capable of?

Hennesey belched out loud, knowing he didn't want to find out. "Think it's time for you to leave, buddy," was his inane response to the situation. "You better move it, and get on out of here."

At first there was shocked silence, the bully barely sparing him a glance. "Who the hell are you?" he said, spitting on the ground, his opinion of Hennesey quite clear. "Like you're gonna do anything," he taunted. "Get out of here. You're not invited to this party!"

"Yeah, yeah," returned Hennessey. "I feel for you, man. She talked smack to me too, but is she worth the trouble?"

Hen hoped the 'We're in this together' kind of approach would work, figuring it would be safer in the long run. Then he heard a snort of resentment coming from Ms. Attitude. God Almighty, did she not know when to keep quiet? All he wanted to do was diffuse the situation, and put an end to this farce.

Hennesey waited a moment, hoping the guy would cool off. Hoping the woman would keep her mouth shut.

"Get away from the car, you two," she challenged from the dark. "I've got a knife and I am not afraid to use it."

The big man guffawed like that was the most hilarious thing he'd heard all day. Hen was stunned. Now it was his turn to get pissed. Here he was trying to shut this guy's testosterone off at the tap, trying to prevent an escalation of violence, when the woman in jeopardy wouldn't close her yapper.

Hen worried about the direction this was going. No one seemed to be mulling around in the parking lot yet. "No knife talk, please," he said lightly. "Come on...this is getting ridiculous. It's after midnight for cripes sake!"

Inching closer to the vehicle, he kept one eye on the brute, the other on the she-devil. He could make her out in the darkness, hugging the side of the car, slowly coming closer to him. What the hell was she doing? Did she think she could—

"Ooomphh."

Hennesey saw stars. Then the Milky Way. The bitch had tackled him. Took him down. He couldn't believe it!

His side exploded with pain. He tried to think through it. Concentrate on his training. An indrawn breath was heard. He was ashamed to learn it was his. Think! his brain screamed inside his head.

An unknown female lay sprawled over his body. Check. Her face was an inch away from his. Check. Why were chicks always prettier in the dark?

Damn that one!

He forgot about his wound, his stomach, his job. He could only be aware of her, and the bony hard things that were poking him from her person. Feeling squashed like a bug, he tried to move, every instinct sending out a fresh alarm.

He felt her arms push down. He felt her thighs squeeze. Every movement set off a new kind of ache. One deep inside his groin. One he hadn't felt in months.

He silently cursed, knowing he had no control over the situation, and worse, no control over himself. Never had he felt so conflicted—one part a thinking federal officer, the other, a helpless upended turtle with...Oh, dear God...a hard on.

Hen was furious. How could his own body betray him this way? He squirmed beneath her, knowing it was critical that he do something. Placing his hands above her chest, he pushed hard. 'Defend and Protect' was the internal command, even though his groin was calling the shots.

The waitress shifted her weight, channeling a flood gate of images that were sheer torture for him.

"In your dreams, buddy!" she whispered, before rolling off.

"Isn't she something?" said the big guy, watching, and no doubt waiting his turn.

Feeling like he'd been hit by a two by four, Hen struggled to get up, his left side on fire. The woman was already on her feet, something in her hand, ready to go toe to toe with the beast-man. He had to focus. Assess. Get his damn head out of his crotch. He saw a flash of silver appear in the woman's hand and felt his stomach do a flip. "Put that thing away!" he hissed. He knew firsthand the kind of damage a blade could do.

Arching herself on the balls of her feet, she seemed fearless. Was she out of her mind? he asked himself. She was on an unstoppable mission to kick ass tonight. Hennesey winced at his predicament. He was in no position get between the two.

"You bastard!" she yelled at the car killer. "You had no right to do what you did!"

The big man pointed to her beat up possession. "It's a piece of crap and you know it!" So saying, he made the mistake of bending down, and grabbing handfuls of gravel. "You don't scare me, and I won't be that easy..."

Bad move, dude, thought Hennesey. He heard a heavy thud, hoping it was the knife hitting the ground. In disbelief he watched Ms. Intrepid curl herself into ball and attack head on.

Damn, that had to hurt, seeing the idiot go down just like he did. Just who was this chick? She had better moves than the U.S. Marshal's service training academy.

After a few moments of watching them roll around, playing "Who's On Top?", Hennesey felt woozy. It was beyond ridiculous watching them. It was late. Finally, he could hear people going to their cars. Leaving. Something he wanted to do hours ago.

"What is it with you two?" he barked. "Knock it the hell off before someone calls the cops!"

"Big deal," said the man on the ground, alternately laughing, and groaning, while being punched by five foot five inches of MEAN. "I am a cop!" he said in a muffled whoosh.

Hennesey was floored. "Well. That explains everything! I feel so much better knowing that." Seeing that sarcasm was wasted on them, he played his last trump card.

"Let me introduce myself. Officer H. B. James, U.S. Marshal, at your service." He stood very still, knowing he'd be kissing the grass if he tried to do otherwise.

His words had an immediate effect. Finally, all action stopped, their heavy breathing testimony to their foolishness. "You, and you," he ordered. "Get up and come over by the light."

"Hey! Gorilla-man! Think you can let go of me now?" ordered the female, still not giving an inch.

"What? Oh, sure. Sure. Sorry!" said the man, stung into moving. He stood up, brushing off his pants. "Hey, what the hell's in your bra, anyway?"

Hennesey saw the guy's big hands reach towards her chest, like he had every right to find out. Not again! he fumed. Why couldn't the dumb ass leave her alone?

"Keep-your-paws-off-me!" breathed the woman. She surfaced from the ground, pushing her hair out of her eyes. "You really a cop?" she asked the man backing away from her.

The beast nodded an assent. She walked up to Hennesey, looking at him square in the face. "You really a marshal?" she asked him in a small voice.

"Yes, ma'am," he answered, steadying himself with a long deep breath. "And you are...?" Hen queried politely.

"I... I am so screwed," said the waitress, with a catch in her voice.

Footsteps rushed down the back stairway. An older man ran past the car, past the bad guy brushing off his clothes, and past Hennesey, who was beginning to feel like he was the real victim here.

"Missy Gay, you alright?" asked the man as he took the woman's arm.

Another commotion rent the air as a second man scrambled down the stairs. Hennesey recognized the bouncer coming to the rescue.

"Just say the word, Mr. Woo," the guy said, cracking his knuckles, "and I'll take care of the both of them." The bouncer raised his fist. "Some folks don't know when to leave."

"No, Jake," spoke the woman. "God, no. They are both law officers."

" Ahh, truly?" questioned the elder man. Hennesey surmised he was in the presence of Mr. Woo himself. "Upstairs," the owner said. "We talk. Have tea. Now." The man gave a curt nod to all of them, expecting no argument as he headed back up the stairs.

"No one tells Tank Flannery what to do!" shouted the bull-man.

Hennesey watched in awe as the bouncer picked him up and deposited the idiot at the bottom step. "No one defies Mr. Woo," warned the man.

Hennesey was beat. He didn't think he had the strength to climb the stairs. Telling himself he had to keep a close eye on Ms. Intrepid, he threw out a line. "Ma'am? Would you come over and give me hand?"

She turned to him, eyes huge in her face. "Are you going to arrest me?"

"Should I?" he quipped. "You did attack a federal officer. That's pretty serious." He felt her tremble. "Come on. You going to help me or not?"

"Yes. Of course, but first," she stepped away hurriedly, going to her car, "I have to get my backpack."

Hennesey thought that was weird. What the hell was so important in the bag?

She came back with it and led him gently to the steps. "Did I hit you that hard?"

"Yeah. Yeah, you did. Took the wind right out of my sails."

Hennesey felt about a hundred years old. He was only thirty-three, damn it, and had failed at everything tonight. To make things worse, the spitfire at his side hit him hard in places he didn't want to think about.

She carefully linked her arm in his as they moved forward. He was thankful she didn't flip him like a pancake over the railing.

"I hate tea," grumbled the idiot ahead of them, as he went through the door.

"Shut up and just keep moving," ordered Hennesey. They were in the kitchen, under fluorescent light when he got a good look at her. The darkest of eyes with thick sooty lashes met his. He saw marks and bruises, her pale complexion sporting big red raised markings all over.

"You stupid son of bitch!" he hollered, grabbing the cop by his shirt. "Look what you did to her!"

All heads swiveled to the woman. Totally embarrassed, she put her hands up to her flaming cheeks. Her fingers lightly traced their contours. "Uhh, I don't think it was him," the waitress replied. "I kind of break out when I'm stressed."

"Oh, really?" asked Hennesey. He relaxed the grip on the idiot's shirt, and pushed him. "And what exactly do you do when you're stressed? Destroy other people's property for the hell of it?"

The man blanched, turning as white as the stack of paper napkins beside him.

"Enough," said Mr. Woo, pointing to a table with steaming cups of hot tea already poured. "You, Mr. H. You not look so good. Sit. Please."

For a small man wearing spectacles, the man sure got everyone's attention. And loyalty, Hennesey surmised, as he shuffled to the table and all but fell into his seat.

The night's events had drained him. A cup of fragrant liquid was placed in his hand.

"Drink," ordered Mr. Woo. "You feel better."

"Do as he says," said the bouncer. "He always knows best."

Oh, what the hell, thought Hennesey. Taking a careful sip, he welcomed the taste of lemon and ginger on his tongue. Within moments his stomach eased up. Even the ache on his side lessened. That damn Mr. Woo was something alright. He looked up to say 'thanks' to the man, but found the darkest black-cherry eyes he'd ever seen boring into him.

Hen could not look away. He felt himself being pulled into deep waters, caught up in a current he had no will to fight. Was this night of surprises ever going to end? He waited for her to say something.

"Can I see some ID, please?" she finally asked.

Oh-kay, he thought, a slight smile tugging at him. "Sure. I'll show you mine if you show me yours."

He meant it as a joke but her lips flattened to a straight line. There was something going on with her, he felt it in his bones. He dug out his wallet and flipped it open to the card with the star on it.

She swallowed hard like an egg was stuck in her throat. He poured himself more tea, watching her reach down and root around her things. She came up with a thick white envelope.

"Am I supposed to show you mine too?" asked the idiot.

"Yes!" said Hennesey, thoroughly exasperated. The cop pulled his wallet out for inspection.

"Well. Your name really is...Tank—short for Tankersleigh. How about that?" stated Hennesey, to no one in particular. "Now tell me, what are you going to do about her car?"

"Hell," the butt-head replied, "I guess I'll have to pay for the damages."

"You... guess you'll pay?" Hennesey fixed him with a glare. "Let me lay it out for you. You've got five days to fix her car so it is road worthy." He motioned for Jake to come to the table. "Uh, Jake, get this guy's license, phone number and particulars. He's going to fix Miss Gay's car for her. Isn't that right, Officer Tank?"

The guy didn't dare utter a whimper, or a protest as Jake clamped him in a vice-like grip. "My pleasure," said the bouncer, giving the man a meaningful squeeze. "Come with me. Then we'll take a little walk to your car."

"I have a feeling Jake will see that things get done," smiled Hennesey, taking control, and hoping to lighten the mood. He pulled her papers out of the envelope.

White legal papers, heavy with black ink and underlined words, showed court dates. All bearing the name of Gayanne

Vaughn vs. the State of New York. Like a bell clanging, her name reverberated around the inside of his head.

"Wow. You really are Gay, aren't you?"

"Oh, please," she rolled her eyes. "Not you too." She carefully gathered the documents and tucked them into her bag on the floor. "Why do people assume—" but she stopped in mid-sentence.

This time, Hennesey captured her with his eyes. His elbows were on the table, his hands steepled above his mouth. Watching intently, he waited for her to explain.

"Stop it."

"Stop what."

"You know what. You are creeping me out."

His eyebrows went up a fraction. "What am I doing?"

"You are staring. That's just rude."

Hen burst out laughing. Mr. Woo turned to give them a look but went back to doing kitchen duties. "Me. Rude. That's rich coming from you. Sort of like calling the pot... black, don't you think?"

She tilted her head not breaking her gaze. Her tongue peeked out and moistened her lips.

Hennesey felt a shift in his gut that had nothing to do with an upset stomach. He had to be the biggest idiot on the planet right now, but, God help him, he couldn't walk away from her.

"I'm in trouble," she blurted out.

"Really? Tell me." He observed how her body was doing the talking. Hands were clasped tightly in front of her. The table shook with the tapping motion of her legs underneath. He sensed she was like a rabbit ready to bolt.

"I can't," she answered. "You won't believe me."

She reminded him of midnight; deep, dark and mysterious. She was full of secrets alright, and he wanted to discover each and every one of them.

"That's harsh," he replied, shifting his gaze to his tea cup. He found himself gently chasing the curve of the cup with his finger, tracing its shape, wondering what tracing her would be like. He looked up, catching her eyes upon him. Still.

"How do you know what I'll say?" he asked.

"Your name," she said, shaking her head, shifting gears again. "What's the 'H. B.' stand for?"

A half-hearted smile crossed his face. "Sure you want to know? It stands for Hennesey Blake. Ridiculous, isn't it?"

"Hennesey?" She leaned in a bit. "You mean, like the whiskey?" she asked.

"Yep. My mama's favorite thing. It's just pure accident that I've got the streaky brown hair and amber eyes to match."

Gay looked at him strangely. He'd been on the receiving end of that look before. "Too beautiful for a guy," was what one female told him recently. Then she stabbed him real good to get her point across.

"Enough about me," he countered. "What about you?"

"Promise you won't laugh?"

"Promise," he told her, making a cross above his heart. "Hope to die if I tell a lie!" he teased.

"I was framed—" she began.

Hennesey couldn't stop the crack of laughter coming up. He stifled it as best he could and coughed. But her eyes shot sparks of anger at him, every one like an arrow aimed at his chest. She pushed herself away from the table, struggling to get up. Hen grabbed her hands, preventing the escape.

"Let go of me." She spoke barely above a whisper.

Hennesey wouldn't do it. He forced her to sit down.

"That was terrible of me. Sorry," he said in earnest, gently squeezing her hands. "If you only knew how many times I've been told that."

"Don't flatter yourself," she flashed back, breaking free of his grip. "If you only knew how many times the words, 'I'm sorry' have been said to me, too."

She didn't raise her hand, but Hennesey felt the implied slap none the less.

"Mr. Woo?" she called out.

Her boss came up to the table. "Missy Gay... You need something?"

She smiled up at him. "Mr. Woo, I can't use my car and I need to get out of here. Can you or Jake take me—"

"No," blurted Hennesey, unable to stop himself.

"Pardon me, Mr. Marshal, but what do you have to say to anything?" She pulled her hands free, her waitress glare back in place.

"You are just like the others," she spat at him. She stood up, disgust punctuating her every word. "You don't give damn about me or what the truth is. You only care about your own ass." Those dark as midnight eyes shot daggers at him. "Know what you can do with that badge of yours?"

"Missy Gay!" said Mr. Woo, shocked by her outburst.

Ahhh, thought Hennesey. Her name, the case, had clicked into place in his head. Holy hell. If this was going where he thought it would—

"Mr. Woo, she and I are going to work this out like two adults," he told the older man.

"Over my dead body," Ms. Attitude uttered between clenched teeth.

"Funny you should mention dead bodies. You wouldn't be part of that Securities and Exchange scandal in New York, awhile back, would you?"

That knocked the stuffing out her, he saw. She seemed to crumple, suddenly grabbing for her chair. He started to get up but Mr. Woo was closer, and nudged her back into her seat. Well, damn! That was one hot button he just pushed.

"I get some ice chips," said the old man, pausing to give Hennesey a pointed look before scooting away.

"I swear—I did not kill Simon Blackridge," she said quietly, red blotches blooming anew all over her face and neck. "He was like a father to me."

Hennesey reached out to touch her arm. He was as serious as a heart attack, sensing she was about to reveal something explosive.

"Uncle Simon trusted me. Trusted me above everyone, even his own partner..."

"Christopher Gerrard," he finished the sentence for her,

remembering the case, remembering the headlines of yet another financial institution pilfering millions from innocent clients. The money was still missing. Just what the hell had he stumbled into?

He watched her face, noting every nuance, every movement she made. For a moment she looked crushed, like she was reliving a terrible sorrow. But the marshal in him prevailed. He was not letting up. Or letting her go.

He asked the million dollar question. "So. Where is the money?"

Gayanne Vaughn swallowed, then looked away.

"Here you are," said Mr. Woo with a wet folded dish towel. "Ice inside. You feel better soon." He nodded, satisfied he could leave them alone again.

Hennesey was close, he could feel it. His mind fizzled like champagne, bubbling with the ramifications of this chance meeting tonight. Somehow, the key that could blast the case wide open sat directly across from him. Gayanne Vaughn.

He closed in on the intimate space they shared, hoping she'd open up. "I'll ask you again. What about the missing money?"

Gay wouldn't look at him. Her fingers applied the ice pack to her face, her arms. Finally, Hennesey took the pack away from her, forcing her to look him in the eye.

Her eyes were filled with misery. Damn it, he could tell she was scared. "Tell me. I can help."

"Oh sure you can," she sniffed. "You put up a real good

fight tonight in front of that cop!"

Hennesey acknowledged the hit. "Yeah. Well, about what happened before...." He let the words hang in the air. "I have this wound on my side that's been giving me grief. Been on medical leave about 5 weeks now."

"Oh my God!" she wailed. "And I jumped on you!"

She reacted the way he hoped she would—she felt bad, but even better, she felt guilty. He had to keep pressing her for an answer.

"Last chance kiddo. Where's the money?"

She let out a huge sigh, and closed her eyes. "I think I have it," she confessed.

He almost fell out of his seat. "You mean, like now?"

"Yes, I think it's in the sticks."

"What sticks?" He wasn't sure what she meant. "You mean like 'out in the country' sticks?"

"No." She touched his arm. "As in the sticks in my backpack."

What the—? Hennesey thought she was crazy. But she reached down into her bag on the floor and brought out a small ordinary compact case, the kind you can get in any discount store. It was blue enamel, and flat, almost three inches wide, and five inches long.

He looked at her in total disbelief. "Uhh, Gay? It's just a case."

She looked at him like he was the village idiot.

Again.

"It's in the sticks," she stressed. "The swizzle sticks." She looked around making sure it was just them, and Mr. Woo. She felt around one side of the case and clicked it open.

Nestled in quilted black satin were exquisite glass rods, three on each side, filled with incredible swirls of color and design, the gold and silver threads within making them pop.

"Gay, what the hell is this? They're just pretty glass rods!"

"Uncle Simon loved glass," she whispered. "And he loved gold. He had these specially made. Made me promise to never tell anyone about them." She reached for his hand.

"That guy...the cop? I thought he was one of Gerrard's men. He keeps finding me. I have to leave here, do you understand?" Her body trembled with remembrance. Carefully, she closed the case when he didn't answer. She reached for the backpack and pushed herself away from the table.

"Whoa. Wait...wait, Gay, please. Just a second."

"You can't see them," she continued, "but, I think there are patterns in the glass." She paused and took a deep breath. "I think they are numbers to a Swiss bank account."

Holy crap, thought Hennesey. That explained a lot. Why she was so defensive. And scared. White collar crime with high stakes like this was no joke, and, hell, this one, had literally fallen into his lap.

His brain took a sudden left turn on him. The un-marshal side reared up, showing him an image of a soft and pliant Gayanne cradled between his thighs. A film of sweat broke out on his brow. He had to stop thinking of laps, for God's sake.

"Wow," Hen said, giving in to a desire to clear his throat. "Well, that sure changes things." And, man, did it ever. She'd been charged with the crime of withholding information. With contempt of court. With being a hostile witness. With being an accessory to murder.

And now, they've let her out as bait, he realized. Hennesey knew how the wheels of justice worked. He'd used the same scenario to gather evidence himself. She was alone, she was being tracked, and she was still the female in distress.

Hen raked his fingers through his hair and thought fast. "Look, I've got a proposition for you." Her eyes flashed their fury at him all over again. "Hold on, Gay." He reached for her hand. "Don't look at me like that. Hear me out—Damn it, would-you-let-me-explain?"

He told her he had wheels and connections. That they needed to stick together, get on the interstate, book a room for a while ("Like that's going to happen" she argued), and then head to Virginia, where his grandfather lived. Now was not the time to tell her that his relative was a judge with friends up the Mississippi, in the White House, and beyond.

Gay said a tearful goodbye to Mr. Woo and Jake.

Hen tossed her the keys to his car. "You trust me?" he asked her.

"Not as far as I can throw you," was her answer, as they both got in.

Hennesey knew he didn't have the whole story. She didn't trust him yet, and that was OK. He was sure of only one thing this whole crazy night: he was meant to find her and keep her safe. Outwardly, that was the marshal thing to do, but inside... that was his secret, the one he buried deep in his heart.

For now, Gay had the wheel and was in control. Hennesey leaned back in his seat, for once looking forward to something.

"What the hell are you smiling about?" Gay asked as she turned onto the highway.

"Nothing, really," lied Hennesey, knowing they had a lot of road to cover.

He just hoped it was going to be one long sweet ride.

Rage and Compassion
ANN GREGORY

White hot rage
struggles with compassion.
She slapped me for everything;
She was beaten, for nothing.
She was raised in filth,
and she was locked in mortal combat
with dirt and germs.
Her house was sterile,
and my every move
was an affront to her shrine.
Her creative spirit
was ground to dust.
My creative spirit
was mocked and maligned.
Her many interferences in my life
have enraged me
beyond reason.
Her own parents have never bothered
to call her even once.
Like Saul,
I have slain my thousand enemies;
Like David,
she has slain her ten thousand.
Rage and compassion:

how much greater
must be her rage,
and how much greater
must be my compassion?

The Wish
STACY McKITRICK

PAIGE STOOD IN THE DOORWAY WITH HER MOUTH open. Did someone turn the conference room into Dracula's lair or did they just forget to turn on the lights?

Her coworkers stood sheepishly beside what she could only proclaim as the sea of morbidity. Pushed up against a black-covered wall, the table—now covered with black papier-mâché—contained a black-draped mound, black napkins, black plates, and black plasticware. Dozens of black balloons hovered over the monstrosity. That wasn't even the worst of it. In a bright, blind-me-now white, printed haphazardly along the edge of the tablecloth were two huge numbers—a "4" and a "0" and the words "Over the Hill."

Over the hill was right. Where did the years go? She had been determined to marry young and change her name, but Mr. Right, or Mr. Will Do, never materialized or were just plain unavailable. Being a couple of bookworms, her parents thought it cute to name her Paige because of the way it sounded with their last name of Turner. She'd lost count the number of times someone asked if she'd read any good books lately.

She suppressed a groan. Mindy was so dead. She was supposed to be a friend. Friends didn't do this kind of crap.

Mike brushed in behind Paige. Now there was a guy she'd like to set her sights on, but he fell into the unavailable range. Last she heard he was either married, engaged, or living with someone. Only human resources knew for sure and they weren't sharing.

"Whoa! What the...?" He looked at her and offered an apologetic smile as he leaned in and whispered, "Remind me not to get on her good side."

Paige bit back a laugh. The last thing she needed was more attention. But Mike was right. Being friends with Mindy was definitely a no-no. An enthusiastic coworker, Mindy used any occasion to celebrate. Maybe when she reached forty, she'd realize no one wanted to celebrate that occasion.

"Happy Birthday!" Mindy snatched the material over the mound as if she were uncovering a masterpiece.

Oh God, more black. Paige felt her arteries harden at the sight. A chocolate-frosted sheet cake, fit for a football team and then some, sported two black balloons: one containing a white "4", the other a white "0".

Just shoot me now.

As Mindy lit candle after candle after candle—dear Lord, did she really have forty of the suckers?—the group sang "Happy Birthday," out of sync and off key thanks to Mindy. She screeched at the top of her lungs, apparently wanting to outdo that nun from *Sister Act*. Was covering your ears at your own party uncouth?

"Make a wish!" Mindy sang as she clapped her hands. The woman was seriously having too much fun.

The candles took on a life of their own. Paige glanced at the ceiling. Could she wish for the sprinklers to go off? If she let them burn, she wouldn't have to wait long. Why couldn't Mindy just get a number four candle and a number zero candle and light those? Paige stepped up to the cake. Forty candles were bright, not to mention hot. Her face tightened. Thank goodness she wore her hair in a ponytail today.

Mindy idled up beside her and nudged. "Make it a good one."

Mike rushed up, holding a fire extinguisher. Where'd he get that? Those meaty biceps of his strained against the sleeves of his yellow polo shirt and nearly turned Paige to goo. He shrugged. "Just in case."

Just in case, indeed. She closed her eyes. *I wish to be rescued.*

Maybe she should have been more specific, like, maybe wish for Mike to rescue her or better yet, wish for Mike to take her out. She'd had it bad for him ever since they'd been introduced and he had laughed out loud at her name. Honesty always scored high with her. So did a sense of humor. Even if she wished all that, it's not like they'd come true anyway. Besides the whole "wishes are for children" bit, he was off limits.

She blew and, miraculously, every candle went out. So did the overhead lights.

"Damn. That's some good blowin'. What'd you do? Wish for a power outage?" Mike said as he lowered the extinguisher.

That would have been a good wish, too—lose power, go home. But how the hell had she blown them all out at once?

Was there an open vent somewhere?

"Sorry, that was me." Dawn, the youngest of the bunch, giggled as the lights flickered back to life. "I leaned against the switch."

Mindy handed Paige a piece of cake and a fork. The corner piece? Really? Just looking at the frosting made her teeth hurt. At least she didn't get one of those black balloons. She could imagine spending the rest of the day with grey teeth.

Oh why did her mother raise her to be kind? She forced a smile. "Thanks. You really didn't have to do this."

Mindy clasped her hands and tilted her head. "Of course I did, silly. I couldn't have you celebrate such an occasion all alone now, could I?"

Oh, no, Heaven forbid. Paige glanced at the door. Would anyone notice if she quietly left? If only she'd taken the day off. She could have made a three-day weekend out of the non-event.

"So what did you wish for?" Mike asked, flashing his eyebrows.

What was that about? The crooked little grin he sported almost implied he thought she wished for sex. Crap. That would have been a better wish, too.

"You can't say," Mindy said. "Then it won't come true."

What are we, five? Paige thought.

"What are you, five?" Mike asked.

Mindy frowned and Paige suppressed a laugh. He wasn't making it any easier not to fall for him.

"Could you imagine if birthday wishes really came

true?" Dawn said.

"Then we'd all be millionaires, right?" Paige said.

"Is that what you wished for?" Mike asked, flashing those beautiful green eyes her way. "Money?"

She gave him a look that said "Wouldn't you like to know." At least, she hoped that's the look she gave him. His laughter made it hard to determine. She was kind of out of practice.

"Money wishes don't come true," Mindy said. "Only wishes of non-material things. I hope you didn't waste your wish on money."

Everyone stopped and stared at Mindy. Did the woman really believe wishes came true? Whoo boy!

"So, you partying tonight?" Dawn asked.

Party? Maybe Dawn still enjoyed her birthdays, but Paige gave up partying back in her twenties. Hell, she hadn't even gone out in, what, a year?

If she said no, Mindy would only pounce, any excuse to take her somewhere. Paige could think of better ways to spend her time. Like going to the dentist. Using her fork, she played with the frosting and came up with a lie. "I don't know. My sister is coming over."

"You have a sister? I didn't know that." Mindy said with a mouthful of cake. Even Mike raised an eyebrow.

"She lives out of state." The lies were flowing now. If she stepped outside, would she be struck by lightning? Nah. She couldn't get so lucky.

Mindy's eyes lit up. "Why don't you bring her along?"

"What?"

"To the party. You know—girls night out. It'll be fun."

"Can I call her and get back with you? She might not be interested."

"Why wouldn't she be interested? Isn't she coming out to celebrate your birthday? It's not everyday you turn the big four-oh."

That's right, Mindy. Rub it in. Paige closed her eyes to an impending headache. How the hell was she going to get out of this? "She's not coming to celebrate."

"Then why is she visiting?"

"Geez, Mindy," Mike said. "Nosy much?"

Paige could kiss Mike right there. Oh, but why stop at a kiss. Would people mind if she threw him on the floor and took him? It was her birthday.

Dang it. Now she wished she had wished for that.

Mike managed to get the spotlight off her imaginary sister and turn it toward work. Yeah, she could kiss him all right. The man was a saint. That sexy stubble only made him appear devilish.

By the time Paige finished her God-awful piece of cake, her stomach was churning. The rest of the day should be just peachy. She thanked everyone and helped clean up. When she returned to her tiny cubicle, she collapsed in her chair. Thank God that was over. Now maybe things could get back to normal. Like people ignoring her.

Mindy stopped by thirty minutes before quitting time and dropped off the cake. Did she expect Paige to take it home and eat it all? Even if she liked the cake, gaining two hundred pounds didn't interest her. Guess the dumpster would get dessert tonight.

"So, is your sister really coming over?" Mike asked.

Paige jumped and spun around in her seat. He leaned against the opening of her cubicle looking better than anyone she knew.

Okay heart, you can start beating again. She brought her finger up to her mouth and shook her head.

"Do you even have one?" he whispered.

Again, she shook her head.

Smiling, he walked into her tiny cubicle, flashing teeth a dentist would drool over. The man knew how to take up all the oxygen. Not to mention the space. Why did she have to fall for the untouchable?

He leaned in close, almost like he was going for a kiss. "Can I buy you a drink, then? For your birthday?"

Dang. No kiss. She wouldn't have minded the kiss. His scent, a mixture of man and more man, intoxicated her. Her heart not only started back up, it did a little giddy-up.

But was Mike asking her out or was this some kind of joke? He'd never really looked at her before, at least not that she'd noticed. "Won't your wife mind?"

"Probably, if I was married."

"Girlfriend?"

"Do you want to go or not?"

Well, hell. Was he actually unattached? "I'll go." She pointed to the cake. "Do you know anyone who wants that?"

He raised an eyebrow as if he'd come up with an evil plan and reached for the sugary creation. "I know just the place for it." He started walking away when he looked over his shoulder. "You comin'?"

Shit, yeah. What's thirty minutes? It was her birthday. She quickly shut down her computer, grabbed her purse and followed him to the exit.

Once outside, Mike stopped at the dumpster and tossed the cake inside.

She laughed. "I was going to do that."

"Great minds, huh?" He brushed his hands as if he'd gotten crumbs on them. "You want to be adventurous tonight?"

He stared at her, a devilish glint in those green eyes of his. Was she being smart? How well did she really know the guy, besides knowing he was the hottest guy in the company and he drove the sweetest car on the lot? Taking risks was not her thing and one of the reasons she had made it to forty. Oh, but she'd been careful her whole life and where had it gotten her? Nowhere, that's where. "What did you have in mind?"

The grin on his face outshone the Cheshire cat's. "Can I surprise you?"

What should she say? Sure, as long as it doesn't require us to be naked? Then again, why would she say that? "I'm not going to regret this, am I?"

He put his right hand up in a pledge. "I promise no bad singing or cake. So what do you say?"

No bad singing, no cake, and some time with Mike? It was a dream come true or more precisely, a wish come true.

So why was she hesitating? "You sure you wouldn't rather spend your Friday night with someone else?"

Mike looked at Paige and wondered why he'd waited so long to ask her out. Sure, dating coworkers was kind of frowned upon, but rules had never stopped him before. Weren't they meant to be broken?

And what was with her question. Who wouldn't want to spend their Friday night with her? She might have just turned forty, but the woman had a kickin'-ass figure. Curves every which way. He imagined releasing her ponytail and running his fingers through that mass of blonde hair while he pulled her soft body up against his hard one. Especially one predominantly hard spot.

"If I didn't want to go out with you, I wouldn't have asked."

The smile started slow, hesitant, but once it grew, her face glowed. If they weren't standing in the middle of the parking lot where any coworker could see them, he'd kiss those luscious lips of hers. Hell, he'd almost done it in her cubicle.

"Okay," she said.

Okaaay. He shoved his hands inside his pockets and with a nod of his head, indicated for her to follow. It had been a long time since he'd gone out on an actual date, and never a spontaneous one. Picking up women at bars was just not his thing, never had been.

Yeah, people at work thought he played around. No surprise Paige thought he had a wife or a girlfriend. The rumors ran rampant at work and he never squelched a one. Truth be told, he'd been alone longer than he'd been with someone. His wife of two years passed away more than ten years ago and the thought of experiencing that pain all over again was enough to steer him clear of any entanglements.

Until he met Paige. She was pretty and funny and the sweetest person he knew. She laughed at his jokes and didn't knock him down when he inadvertently cracked up at her name. Yeah, he liked her, but she also scared him. Scared him into thinking he could have another relationship. So what changed? Probably that stupid party. He would have shot Mindy if she had pulled that crap on him four months ago when he turned forty. But seeing Paige's agony set off some macho protective side he didn't even know he had and he wanted to lift her spirits.

It's not like he'd been thinking about her since the party, picturing her in all sorts of positions. Yeah, he hadn't been doing that at all.

He opened the passenger door to his Mustang GT, but before he could get out of the way, she rubbed up against him, her hand conveniently brushing one particularly sensitive part. Hot damn. Best touching he'd had in ages. She made him feel like a randy teenager and he swallowed down a groan. She smelled good enough to eat. He couldn't wait to get her alone.

He knew the perfect place, too. A place where no one could interrupt them.

Paige stared out the window of the Mustang and fiddled with the strap on her purse. Had she lost her mind? Had she actually groped Mike? She certainly didn't expect to feel his erection. Heck, she never expected he'd get one for her.

After what seemed like a long time for him to walk around the car—probably adjusting himself—he slid behind the wheel. Suddenly, the inside of his car felt more like a muggy summer in Florida than the dry one in Southern California. He was either one hot man or she was experiencing her first hot flash.

After a pleasant drive where she stuck to safe subjects like work, he took the exit for the marina and parked the car in the lot.

"We here for the restaurant?" She'd heard it was pretty good.

He unbuckled his seatbelt. "Nope. My brother and I own a boat. Thought I'd take you for a ride. You don't get sea sick, do you?"

A boat? He has a boat? On the water? She gripped her purse handle. "I don't know. Does this boat have life jackets?"

"What does that have to do with getting sea sick?"

"Nothing. It'll make a difference whether or not I go on the boat."

He furrowed his brow. "You don't swim?"

Now her embarrassment would reach an all-time high. "Go ahead. Make jokes about how a forty-year-old, living on the coast, doesn't know how to swim."

"Didn't you have to take swimming in school? I did."

"Yeah, well, I got a C. What can I say?"

Mike chuckled. "Don't worry. I have life vests, not that I plan on throwing you overboard. But if you'd rather not..."

"No, as long as you have the vests, I'm good." If she drowned, at least she spent her last few hours with her dream guy.

She climbed out of the car and followed him down to the docks. While passing by every type of boat, she prayed Mike's towered over them all. She might have to rethink this adventure if he had one a good wave could knock over.

He stopped halfway down the dock. "So, what do you think?"

The boat was, well, huge. Designed for a party of people, it was completely gas-powered, no sails to knock her overboard. She was feeling safer already.

He walked onto the back platform—something he called a swimmer's deck—causing the boat to bounce, unlocked a door, then returned and offered a hand.

The deck lay close to the water without any kind of hand railing, but she refused to act like a chicken. She took his warm hand and gingerly stepped on the platform, wishing there was something she could grab, besides him, and quickly slipped through the little door.

"The life vests are downstairs," he said. "Go grab one and explore. I'll be right back."

"Where are you going?"

"I have a small errand to run."

"You're leaving me alone with your boat?"

He flashed that pearly white smile. "You plan on stealing it?"

She couldn't let him see her fear even though it pretty much ruled her at the moment. "Of course. Why else do you think I'm here?"

With one raised eyebrow, he leaned in close. "To be adventurous. Right?"

Just stepping on the boat was pretty adventurous for her. Again, she thought he might kiss her; instead, he grinned and hopped onto the dock, leaving her alone on the boat.

She climbed downstairs and placed her purse on the table. The lower level contained almost anything anyone would need to live on the boat, including a bed. What kind of adventures did he have in mind?

She found the life vests. She supposed it slipped over her neck, but thought it'd be a lot more fun if he put it on her. Hell, maybe he didn't even plan on taking the boat out. The place was fairly quiet and definitely private. Better than any restaurant or bar.

Paige returned to the top. Another boat passed on its way out to the ocean. Tiny waves rocked her and she grabbed onto a seat. Maybe she should wait on the dock. It wasn't liable to pitch her into the water. Well, neither was the boat, but at least the dock didn't move.

She gripped the boat and carefully stepped from the swimmer's deck back onto the wooden, steady world. What a wimp. Mike would probably think her insane and if he held any kind of romantic ideas, she was sure to have squelched them once he saw her quivering on the dock.

Who knew her wish would come true with that stupid cake? She had wished to be rescued, and Mike had basically done that already. He'd saved her at the party and he'd done it by asking her out. Being alone was the pits. So why was she ruining a granted wish by looking like a scared child?

Paige eyed the boat. Ropes secured it to the dock. It wouldn't float off and the sides were high enough, she shouldn't fall over, especially if she stayed below. If it rocked, she'd pretend she was on one huge water bed. Yeah, that's it. However, getting back inside the boat, now that would take some guts. Not to mention steady feet. She wasn't sure she owned either.

After a deep breath, or five, she stepped onto the little platform just as another boat sped on past. Wasn't there some kind of speed limit in these places?

The boat pitched and she lost her footing. She flew backward and hit the water. A sudden coldness gripped her and she gasped, taking in a mouthful of the salty ocean. Spitting and coughing, she fought to stay afloat, but panicked when her feet couldn't touch anything solid. Her heart pounded in her ears. Where was the boat? Where was the dock? She reached out and only touched water. She was too far away.

Oh God. Was this the end?

An arm came around her chest. "I got you, Paige. Take it easy."

Mike's voice sounded like heaven. She grabbed his arm and tried to relax. Really, she did. When did he jump in? Hell, did it matter? He swam her to a ladder to the dock and she grabbed on for dear life. Unfortunately, her panic attack refused to let her move. Shivering, she hugged the ladder and panted, so thankful to be alive.

"You're okay, Paige. Go on up."

Up. Yeah, up was good. She grabbed the rung and pulled. Did the same with the next one. Mike followed close behind, offering words of encouragement. When she reached the top, she nearly kissed the dock. Wouldn't have been too hard, she was lying facedown.

Next thing she knew, Mike sat beside her and pulled her into a hug. His hard body felt more than good and she hugged him back, needing something solid to hold onto.

"Oh God, Paige. Are you hurt?"

He rubbed her back and head as if he was making sure she was for real. Even his voice sounded urgent. Who was panicking now?

"Was this part of the adventure?" she asked. "If so, I think I'll pass."

His chuckle made her smile and made her feel even better. "Too scary? Then I'll scratch it." He moved her back a bit and stared into her eyes. "Are you really okay?"

"Wet, cold, freaking out, but not hurt. Thank you, by

the way." The words seemed inadequate for what he had done. She was about to suggest they get off the dock when he cupped her face.

"I'm just glad I showed up in time. I thought I'd lost you, too."

Too? Who else had he lost?

"I want to..." He left the words hanging out there as he stared at her mouth.

"You want to what?"

"Do this." He planted his lips on hers and kissed her. Urgent and hungry, his tongue sought entrance and she obliged, tasting him as he explored her mouth. Heat flared and her shivers stopped. She brought her arms up, wrapped them around his neck and kissed him back.

If she'd known kissing Mike was akin to Heaven, she would have wished for that.

He pulled back and flashed his eyebrows. "Why don't we go inside and get out of these wet clothes."

Wow. Now there was an invitation she would not refuse. Whatever magic those birthday candles held made this her best birthday ever. Seemed all her wishes had come true.

Titanic Love

LINDA CHALK

TITANIC LOVE IS THE RETELLING OF FAMILY LORE IN-terwoven with actual events. Eva and Stefan were real people with a real story. Like so many immigrants in the early 20th century, they left their homeland in Eastern Europe to start a new life in America.

April 10, 1912, Cherbourg France

Eva stared into the endless press of waiting passengers, plain brown or black suitcases held to one side, duffle bags flung over their shoulders. The smell of crisp salty sea hung thick and low. In search of scraps, birds squawked overhead and dove almost drunkenly toward the vessels.

"Mama, is that the boat?" Yosef pointed through a tunnel of legs toward the vessel tied to the dock with thick ropes. "You said it was a big boat."

"That's the tender, Yosef," she answered her oldest son. Just eight, he was always inquisitive, as boys his age were. "The big ship is anchored beyond the sea wall."

"A tender?" He scrunched up his nose as if having tasted a piece of bad beef.

"The water is too shallow here. Traffic will ferry us to the big ship."

Crew members shouted orders in a fluid language she could not understand. With a clang of steel against steel the gangway reached out to greet the voyagers.

Finally. They would soon depart this continent and embark on a new journey.

It was with melancholy she was leaving her homeland, not knowing if she would ever return. But dear sweet Stefan was waiting for her across the sea.

Two years ago in 1910 Stefan had first sailed to America to find work and make his fortune to start a better life for his family. Eva had last seen him about a year ago; that's when... She felt the heat of her blush as she stared down at the tiny bundle beginning to stir in her arms. Michael was now one month old. A difficult pregnancy had kept her from joining her husband in America earlier.

"When can we see Daddy?" Four-year-old Sophia tugged at her mother's skirt. She seemed to think their trip would be a short boat ride across the bay. They had already traveled many miles from their home in Hungary to Cherbourg, France, where *Titanic* would deliver them to New York.

"Daddy," three year old Maria echoed, and cuddled her rag doll to her face.

They all missed their father and were losing patience waiting in the seemingly endless line. Already *Titanic* had been delayed by more than an hour and a half. Some incident with another liner at the port of departure—Southampton, she'd heard.

"Yosef, take your sisters' hands." With her own free

hand, Eva dragged the small crate a few more feet toward the waiting boat, and then took a seat upon it with a sigh. Maria crawled onto her lap.

"It's my turn," Sophia whined.

"Is not," Maria snapped.

"Girls, hush," Eva scolded.

She knew she was probably foolish to have brought the set of heavy dishes—she'd sold nearly all their possessions—but she needed something familiar to start up housekeeping. Everything else in the crate was small personal items for the trip. Third class passengers could only bring what they could carry. And with four children, including and a babe in arms, she could take very little.

"Are we almost there?" Yosef asked.

"I don't know, Yosef." She fought to contain her irritation.

Eva moved a few more steps forward, dragging the heavy crate of green dishes. Michael was light in her arms, but they grew weary with the weight. Her two daughters scrambled to be the first on her lap. The older Sophia won. If the crate didn't make a good seat, she would question her own sanity for bringing it.

She noticed then Yosef shuffling against her restlessly. "I have to go pee," he said.

"You'll have to hold it, Yosef."

The flow of people finally broke loose and they began to move forward.

"Mama, I have to go pee." He was now holding himself

and crouching over.

"There is no place, Yosef. Take your sisters' hands." Anxiety spread through Eva like tingly shards.

Michael screwed his face up to cry.

"I can't wait, Mama."

Yosef looked back toward the terminal. Then he was gone, swallowed up by the crowd.

April 14, 1912, New York, New York

Stefan arrived in New York after his long journey from Hamilton, Ohio. He was physically exhausted from the trip and eager to clean up, but the thought of seeing his beautiful Eva in a few days somehow revitalized him. He could only wonder at his wife's stamina—the long journey across the North Atlantic, four children in tow, little Michael he'd never seen. Stefan swelled with pride at Eva's undertaking. After checking into the hotel and eating a small dinner, he retired for the evening.

The next morning, refreshed from a night of uninterrupted sleep, Stefan strolled to the hotel lobby and breakfast amongst a hubbub of current news events. He couldn't help but tune into the chatter as he waited in line to be seated in the dining room. The words sent chills down his arms and spread into tingling fingers.

She struck an iceberg. The *Virginian* reported blurred signals. Abrupt silence.

A business man dressed in suit and tie said to another, "Word is she flashed out wireless calls for help."

"Weren't Mr. and Mrs. Isidor Straus supposed to be on board *Titanic?* You know them, don't you?"

Stefan felt the blood drain from his face. *Titanic?* "Where did you hear this?" he asked the men.

"I've done business with Mr. Straus."

"No. I mean about *Titanic.*"

"It's all over the morning papers," a man behind him answered and unfolded the front page of a New York paper to show him.

TITANIC HITS ICEBERG

Stefan grabbed the paper. Since English was not his first language, he scanned what he could of the story. The *Carpathia*, southeast of the *Titanic* by about 58 miles, picked up the distress call and began sailing to location where *Titanic* was last heard.

"Do you know someone on board?"

Stefan could only nod. A great weight descended upon his shoulders.

"The paper reports she's injured but safe," the man behind him said.

The pieces didn't make any sense to Stefan. *Last signals from* Titanic *were late last night, a few blurred signals ended abruptly.* That didn't sound like *Titanic* was safe. His stomach recoiled. His appetite gone, he relinquished his place in the dining room line and left the hotel.

Anxiety needled Stefan into action. He had to do something. Anything. He was not a man to stand by idle as the world circled around him—he had taken charge of his life to seek out a new and better future for his family in America. Stefan got directions to the White Star Line office on Broadway.

Automobiles, wagons, and other conveyances rattled past as he navigated the city streets. Faces of strangers blurred and blended. Life in the city appeared normal, but his world was collapsing beneath his feet. Isolation swept over him. His longing to be reunited with his family rose in magnitude with every step. And every step brought them no closer. As he slipped into the shadow of a tall building, a cold April wind hit his chest and made him shiver. He pulled the collar of his thin coat up to his chin and braced himself against the cold. Another gust swept up paper and debris to swirl within the corridor of towering monoliths.

A crowd had already gathered at the White Star Line office, demanding answers. They varied from upper crust society, dressed in hats and feathers, to the modestly attired immigrants, who like him, had family traveling in third class. A group of reporters was in the process of questioning the company's vice president, Phillip Franklin.

"There is no danger that *Titanic* will sink," Philip Franklin reported. "The boat is unsinkable and nothing but inconvenience will be suffered by the passengers."

"But some say she foundered."

"Go back home, or to a hotel, or wherever you are staying. You can meet *Titanic* at pier 59 on Wednesday." The vice president dismissed the crowd and the reporters and closed the door to his office.

Stefan rejoined the bustle of activity on the streets of New York, wanting to be soothed by the message of the White Star Line executive. Alone and silent, his thoughts carried his feet forward. The line into the dining room had cleared so he paused to take in nourishment.

Restless energy kept him moving, so Stefan wandered back onto the streets in search of more news. He managed to find his way to the White Star Pier 59 and again came upon others desperate to separate out the facts of *Titanic's* fate from the rumors. So far, news had only trickled in with no reliable way to separate the two. Reassurances continued throughout the day that passengers had been safely moved to the Allan liners *Parisian* and the *Virginian*, which was towing the *Titanic* into port. As the hours passed, the general mood remained optimistic and indicated a favorable outcome. But for Stefan, whose entire world was on that ship, doom clawed at his heart.

The following day, April 16, Stefan returned to the White Star Pier 59. When he caught a glimpse of *Titanic's* photo on the front page of the *New York Times*, he dug into his pocket for a penny and handed it to the paper boy.

TITANIC SINKS FOUR HOURS
AFTER HITTING ICEBERG

The headline was a punch to his gut; he doubled over.

Stefan struggled to extract every meaningful detail he could translate. Making any sense of the story was a dizzying ride of emotional highs and lows.

At 11:36 the *Titanic* wired the White Star liner *Olympic* that they were putting the women and children into life boats. Captain Haddock of the *Olympic* later sent a wireless reporting that when the *Carpathia* reached the position where *Titanic* had collided with an iceberg all they found were lifeboats and wreckage.

The lump in Stefan's throat might as well have been a noose. He couldn't swallow. He couldn't breathe. *Wreckage...* He thought he had given his family a great gift. *Titanic* had been publicized as the world's largest, safest, most luxurious five-star floating hotel. How could she have hit an iceberg and sunk?

1,250 probably perished; noted names missing.

The words blurred and began to swim in front of him.

At 8:20 last night the once extremely optimistic Phillip Franklin conceded that probably only those passengers picked up by the *Carpathia* had been saved. The current figure was 866. He could not provide a number for the total loss of life. Until they heard from the Allan liners *Virginian* and *Parisian* there was still hope that the messages from Halifax were true; the passengers had been dispersed in several vessels.

There was no point in continuing to read through eyes that could no longer focus. He sat down on the dock and leaned against the terminal, its cold brick and concrete walls like steel knives in his back. Another man reading the same paper nearby slumped forward. He wiped tears from his eyes and returned to a straight posture as though putting together the pretence of bravery.

"My brother, Sven. He traveled in steerage. He was coming to help my bakery."

"I'm sorry," Stefan said.

"You?" the man asked.

"My wife Eva, and four children. Michael is only..." His voice cracked before he could swallow his despair. "One month. I have yet to meet Michael."

"Wife and children... Then you still have hope."

"There is always hope," Stefan said.

Stefan dragged through the next couple of days in a dull lethargy, as if events were happening to someone else. He was bone weary; his legs, like lead weights he could not shed. The restless, sleepless nights were beginning to take their toll. Crevices were forming beneath dark sinking eyes. His shoulders slumped from the burden he carried.

Each day he wandered back to the White Star Pier 59 seeking news. The published list of survivors was only a partial. And all of them were in first class, including J. Bruce Ismay, President of the International Mercantile Marine, the corporation that owned *Titanic*. Since no names of third class passengers were listed, rumors abounded that all those in steerage had perished.

A haggard looking man, not so different from himself, complained, "How is it that Ismay survived? The captain went down with the ship. My wife was on *Titanic!* Whose place did Ismay take on that lifeboat?" The man broke down and sobbed.

Stefan could not answer. It was not for him to judge.

April 18, 2012, New York Harbor

At 9:00 p.m. the *Carpathia* arrived in New York Harbor in the pouring rain. A gusty wind made the drops feel more like pellets of steel. A flotilla of boats with newspaper reporters followed the liner into the harbor. Thousands of people waved as the *Carpathia* passed. She floated up the Hudson River and past her own pier. At the White Star Pier 59 she dropped off *Titanic's* empty lifeboats. Random flashes of lightening illuminated the drama. Once the lifeboats were unloaded, *Carpathia* made her way back to her own Pier 54 where the passengers of *Titanic* would disembark.

Stefan waited in the area designated for friends and relatives of survivors. Sobs and shouts went through the crowd as one by one, in agonizingly slow motion, he watched *Titanic's* first and second class survivors reunite with relatives and friends. The eerie wails of the crowd grew louder and louder and swept over the pier like a mighty wave. Reporters shouted out questions that most refused to answer.

Some survivors stopped to reveal conditions on their rescue ship, and praised the *Carpathia's* crew and passengers for how well they were fed and clothed. The ill had been cared for by doctors.

The stories of screams, endless pleas for help from those struggling in the water, heart rending tales of leaving loved ones assaulted Stefan and fueled his terror.

"I thought we'd never get through the ice field. The icebergs were large and the air terribly cold," a young female passenger commented to a reporter.

"What was it like when you hit the water?" a zealous reporter shouted at a man wrapped in a blanket.

"Like a thousand knives severing every nerve in my body," the man answered bitterly.

For two hours Stefan watched the first and second class survivors step from the canopied gangway and weave their way through the gauntlet of customs officers: crewmen, ladies of esteem with bags of jewels, others with only their night clothes. Most walked by their own power, but some were carried and taken to the ambulance corps waiting nearby.

Finally, the third class survivors disembarked. Divided between anticipation and dread Stefan studied each face in the crowd. Some of the women were without wraps and children with very little clothes. Only by sheer willpower did he remain upright on exhausted, rubber-like legs. He'd been standing on the pier for hours and on an empty stomach. Vertigo threatened to topple him. Many eyes glanced his way as they too sorted through those anxiously waiting at port. Faces blurred and mingled into visions of Eva. His heart lurched each time he thought he'd spied his beloved, until he began to question his own sanity. One by one the survivors passed until the *Carpathia* had emptied. Alas, there was no ending his pain....

Three days passed in a never ending grip of helplessness and despair. A cold heaviness clutched his heart. It was as if some force compelled him to spend his days at the pier watching ships come and deposit their cargo and passengers and then recede into the distance. As if by leaving the pier, he would be giving up on his family.

What else could he do? What else could he have done?

Regulars at the pier—vendors, reporters, employees—flashed pity in their eyes as they passed. He knew they thought he was mad.

The tears no longer formed as visions of his beautiful Eva and Yosef and Sophia, sweet Maria and little Michael tumbled before him. Their cries of terror as they drifted to the bottom of the sea haunted him. What nightmares had they endured? They had no doubt witnessed others fill the limited space in lifeboats. It must have been like a death sentence to watch as boat after boat was pushed off from the side, Eva doing her part to quell the children's fears. The ship must have groaned and shivered as it strained to stay afloat. And then with *Titanic's* last gasp what unfathomable agony to be sucked into the icy waters of the North Atlantic?

"Go home." A maintenance worker bumped him with his broom.

Pulled from his grim world, Stefan sat up from where he sat pressed against the hard brick wall.

"The *Parisian*, *Virginian* or any other ship ain't picked up no more survivors."

Stefan knew it was time. He had to return to his job and his apartment in Hamilton Ohio. The apartment he had so lovingly prepared for his family's homecoming.

There was nothing more he could do.

April 22, 1912, New York, New York

The liner *Rochambeau* floated into New York harbor. She drifted pass the famous landmark of welcome and hope, the Statue of Liberty. No one gazed at the tall lady without some outward emotion. Some knelt at the railing and prayed thanks for health and safe passage. Others gazed through glassy eyes with apprehension. America. Through their fatigue, others cheered with excitement. Children sat on shoulders, wide-eyed to get a better view of the statue they had heard so much about.

"Look Mama," her eldest called out, pointing at the famous lady. "It's the liberty!"

Tears flowed easily from Eva's eyes as the *Rochambeau* drifted pass Liberty Island. Sophia and Maria pressed their faces against the railing to peer out. Eva struggled to smile at her son, who was bubbling over with excitement at the long anticipated landmark. And the lady did not disappoint. But apprehension knotted inside Eva. She had for many years eagerly prepared her family's arrival. But the thought of Stefan…. A pain squeezed her heart. She ached to reach out to him, to have him beside her, swinging her into his arms. She held tightly to the vision of his face, of his strong shoulders. Eva had heard the news of *Titanic*. What monstrous nightmares had Stefan envisioned, thinking them swallowed by the sea?

How would she ever find him? She felt so lost in this big wide country, the size of which she could not comprehend. And despite all these people around her, cheering and crying, she felt totally alone. Would Stefan be at Ellis Island? Would he be waiting for them?

Early May, 1912, Hamilton Ohio

A persistent knock on his door awoke Stefan from his slumber. In a groggy stupor he stumbled out of bed, annoyed that his so carefully designed routine was being disrupted. A permanent sorrow weighed him down to where his life had become a mere existence. He rose in the morning, spent his day at the foundry, and his evening alone in his apartment. He then retired to bed and so it began again. His world had shattered and like the debris of the fallen *Titanic*, it had disappeared into the depths of the icy North Atlantic. Everything he had lived for was gone. Only raw sores remained of what had once been a joyous heart.

"Who is it?" he growled as he stumbled through the dark kitchen toward the apartment entrance. It must be important for someone to bother him at this late hour.

"I'm with the Red Cross," the voice answered.

With a tired, shaky hand, he opened the door. The bulb illuminating the hall seemed unusually bright and hit him in the face. He squinted and blinked though sleepy eyes at the dark figures standing in the hallway. Was he dreaming? When the tiny voice of Sophia calling "Daddy" broke through his mind he noticed the pained sobs coming from his own throat.

The woman in worn, dark clothes rushed forward and he embraced her, little Michael, whom he'd never met sandwiched between them. Eva's body trembled with jagged sobs. Her warm tears moistened his neck.

"Eva, Eva." He smothered her face with kisses. "I thought you were... dead," he choked. By some miracle, his family had been returned. And the warmth and light that had died within him was restored.

"Daddy," little Sophia said. And three sets of arms came around his legs. His family.

The Red Cross woman, who had escorted his family here, slipped into the shadows of the hallway and disappeared.

Stefan chuckled and pulled away from Eva. "Yes. I'm here, Sophia. Let me take a look at you." The three sets of arms released him so he could bend down. "My, you've grown. And you, Yosef and Maria." A lump caught in his throat as he stood to gaze at the face of the tiny son he had never seen.

"Michael...."

Eva passed the bundle to her husband. He smiled down at his son, who gazed back through large brown eyes. When Stefan grabbed the leather handle of the crate to bring it inside, he noted the heaviness of its weight. How had Eva dragged it all the way from Hungary? He looked back at her, the corners of his mouth curling up.

Inside their new home, the children curled up on the big sofa, content to again have their family whole. As their mother told of their misadventure, they quickly dozed off. She told how Yosef had stepped out of the line to the tender boat to go pee. By the time they returned, the big ship *Titanic* was pulling away.

"I was very angry with Yosef at the time. Missing the boat was a great inconvenience."

Stefan studied her face through the dim lamp light— the deliberate way her fine lips formed the words in their native language.

"We had to travel from Cherbourg, France to LeHavre, where we boarded the *Rochambeau*. It wasn't until we were on the *Rochambeau* that we heard news of the sinking of *Titanic*. I knew you would think us dead. And I was so worried about you." She wiped away tears.

She had to be exhausted, bone weary. But her strong will and self reliance revealed itself in the way she sat tall and proud in the arm chair across from him.

Eva went on to explain how the people at Ellis Island helped them. "There were interpreters. But the Red Cross took all this time to find you."

He placed the sleeping Michael on the couch with his siblings. Then he went to his wife and held out his arms for her. She stood and molded herself to him.

"I'm so sorry Eva. I know it couldn't have been easy for you with four children and all your worldly possessions in tow." He glanced down at the crate. There wasn't much, but it was all they had from their homeland.

"It doesn't matter now." She looked at him with clear eyes that sparkled of love. "We are together again, in America."

"Tomorrow, you can put away your dishes and arrange things the way you like. Make this apartment feel like home." He kissed her on the forehead and held her close, breathing in her scent. "I've put money aside, so you can go shopping for some necessities." His words brought a smile to her face.

He continued to gaze at her intently. Then his mouth was on hers, stoking a growing fire within them both—Eva responded with her own demand—two pounding hearts lost in the intimate moment.

Eva pulled away and gasped, "Stefan, the children."

"I think they'll be fine." He winked. Then he swept his wife, weightless, into his arms.

"Wha... what are you doing?" she stammered.

"I'm carrying you over the threshold." Then he carried her into the room they would share, and eased her gently onto the bed.

The Death of Harry

ANN GREGORY

CARMEN HAD WORKED FOR OHIO STATE Healthways for over fifteen years. In that time a lot of people had come and gone. Some of them she'd liked and had been sad when they left. Others she'd been ambivalent about. There had been a few she'd disliked enough to celebrate when they left.

Then the company hired Harry, and Carmen learned she was capable of a whole new level of loathing.

Harry was loud, obnoxious, and rude. If he didn't like someone's dress or tie, he said so.

But in Carmen's opinion Harry's biggest problem was that he was too darn good at his job. He could fix any problem, answer any question, and charm any customer. There was no way the company would get rid of him. He was too valuable.

Carmen's own boss, Mr. Dillman, told her all the bosses were aware of the way Harry bullied his coworkers, and they had spoken to him about it on several occasions, stopping just short of threatening him with firing. But their words had no impact on Harry—he simply shrugged them off. And the bosses were at a loss as to what to do next.

Although Harry picked on everyone, he seemed to particularly focus on Carmen. Thirteen years younger than she was, Harry took joy in making disparaging remarks on everything from her clothing to her hairstyle to her makeup. She felt the sharp barb of his tongue often, and it took its toll.

One night Carmen dreamed about killing Harry. She woke up and, strangely, didn't feel guilty. In fact, she laughed.

As it happened there was a staff meeting scheduled that morning. Normally Carmen dreaded staff meetings, but today, she didn't mind.

She put on a dress she hadn't worn since Harry's public comment that the dress was ten years out of style and its color completely unflattering. Today, she didn't care. Today, she was going to kill Harry.

Everyone was already in the meeting room when she got there. When she entered, Harry turned to her and said, "I'd hoped you'd burned that rag. It's such an eyesore we shouldn't be subjected to it."

There was a lot of shifting of weight and squeaking of chairs, and no one but Harry would meet her eyes. Of course he had skewered the rest of them, too, and they didn't want to interfere, lest he turn on them.

Today, instead of cowering, Carmen smiled. "I dreamed about you last night, Harry."

"Yeah, well that's the only place you'll get near me, Carmen, is in your dreams." He said it without even a sneer. As if she was that unimportant.

"You flatter yourself. In my dream, I killed you, Harry."

Suddenly everyone's head snapped up to look at her. Even Harry's attention was on her.

"Oh? How did you do it?" His expression was one of mild curiosity.

Everyone's eyes were riveted on her now, including Mr. Dillman.

"Well, one day in a staff meeting you said something particularly cruel, and I leaped across the table and choked you to death. As sympathetic as my coworkers were, they had all seen me do it, so I was arrested.

"I exercised my right to be tried by a trio of judges instead of a jury of my peers. After the prosecutor presented all the evidence, even my own lawyer told me it was hopeless.

"The judges left the courtroom, but they returned after only a few minutes. They each held up a card. The first judge held up a ten, the second one a nine, and the third one another ten.

"My lawyer said, 'You're giving her twenty-nine years?'

"'Twenty-nine years?' I shouted. 'If you had only known Harry...'

"The judges all laughed. 'No, that's your score. You got two tens for killing Harry.'

"'But why the nine?' I asked.

"'For not killing him sooner. You see, we all knew Harry.'"

There was a stunned silence and then the room erupted in laughter. Everyone roared except Harry, whose cheeks turned red.

One of the other staff members said, "If you choked him and I saw it, I would tell the police it was self-defense."

"Me, too!"

"Justifiable homicide!"

Suddenly Mr. Dillman held up a sheet of paper. Everyone turned to look. It had the number ten written on it in large lettering. Again everyone roared.

Mr. Dillman looked at Harry and said, "You've had that coming since you got here, Harry. I was just wondering who would be the one to step up. Congratulations, Carmen. And by the way, I love that dress."

Harry never bothered Carmen again.

Sam, Kate, and the Lunch Lady's Secret
Dakota James

CRIME SCENES ARE USUALLY THOUGHT OF AS BEING in dark alleys, homes, night clubs. Real life is not prime time television—crime happens everywhere, including Sunny Valley School. Even here, police tape attracts attention; the crowd was just younger than usual.

Lunch lady Mildred stood outside the industrial sized freezer babbling, repeating her story to anyone who would listen to her. "It started with the ice cream. They took the ice cream, all the tubs of ice cream."

Detective Sam Wyatt wished for the twenty-seventh time that morning that he still smoked. Wait, no, he was up to twenty-nine times. He forgot that near miss he had on the way to work just a few hours ago on Columbia Parkway when some freaking yuppie on a cell phone darn near clocked him during an illegal lane change. If it hadn't been raining so hard, Sam would have pulled the suit over and hauled his ass out of his ridiculously large Beamer just for the hell of it. But, no. He didn't feel like starting the day soaked to the skin because of a traffic stop in the rain. Damn, he hated it when it rained in Cincinnati. Turned traffic into a real cluster.

And if that wasn't annoying enough—because, seriously, young urban professionals on cell phones in expensive European cars just really pissed him off—once he got to the station, just when he thought things could not get any worse, he learned his new partner assignment. Kate Tyler. Kate-who-did-not-know-what-she-did-to-him-Tyler.

Great.

Just freaking great.

He knew once he started hearing Bogey in his head, "Of all the gin joints in the world, she had to walk into mine," that he was in for a long day. So, yeah. Watching dear, sweet lunch lady Mildred babble on and on about ice cream made him long for tobacco. And the kind of crime scene that he had to organize and process, such as a school cafeteria, made him jones for loose-leaf tobacco. The kind he would use to roll his own smokes.

IF he was a smoker, that is. None of those pansy store-bought cigs for him. Oh, HELL no! He wanted tobacco so strong it would make him darn near high from the intense nicotine hit he'd get from the first puff of the forbidden smoke.

If only.

Holy shit, Sam. Shaking his head, he heard his little voice badgering him, Nut UP, Sam. Soon you'll be sighing like a little girl.

No, Sam wasn't sure what was worse, having the ever-beautiful, babe-a-licious Kate Tyler for a partner, or working a crime scene where he knew his CSI unit would turn up prints on hundreds of unknown subjects.

Who was he kidding? Truth be told, he wasn't all that wild about the fact that he was hearing voices in his head, either. And he despised crime scenes involving schools or kids.

Mildred was kicking it into high gear, though, because she kept saying over and over, "They stole the ice cream! They stole the ice cream!"

Sam's patience was about shot and it wasn't even noon yet. And, Mildred's babbling was darn near on his last nerve. He looked around the scene and saw a uniformed officer standing near the door. He waved him over and told him, "Talk to that woman and take her statement. Maybe she'll stop saying the same thing over and over." The uniformed cop gave him a glare that clearly said, "Gee, thanks, Detective", before nodding his acceptance of Sam's order and stamping towards Mildred.

"How many people do you think come through this room in a single day, boss?" Sam's junior detective in his squad, John Quinn, asked him as he jotted down a few notes in his notepad.

John's question drew Sam's attention back where it belonged, to the business at hand. Sam didn't say anything for a moment. Liking how John approached a crime scene, Sam realized the kid knew what he was doing. He seemed a natural in assessing crime scenes.

Sam turned to look around the cafeteria, evaluating the room size, gauging how many tables and seats would fit in the room, and estimating how many kids might cycle through the room for lunch. "Maybe eight or nine hundred? Hard to say." Taking note of a man with the stamp of a school principal all over him, Sam jerked one thump in his direction and said, "Let's start with a list of adults who work in the cafeteria, as well as any parent volunteers and see what pops out of that. Let me know when you get that info." John nodded and walked over to talk to the principal. Sam's right hand reached for the inside pocket of his suit.

"I thought you gave up smoking? Or have you given up on that commitment, like all your other commitments?"

OH PERFECT. The voice of the person he'd been off-and-on thinking about for the past few hours was not only in his head, but seemed to be an incessant buzzing in his ear, like bees following you around at a picnic.

How appropriate. Equating Kate to a bee. She tended to sting most everyone she came in contact with.

Well, men anyway.

Keee-rist, Sam. Get a grip.

He really wasn't in the mood for this today. Craving tobacco AND Kate all in the middle of a crime scene? In a frigging school?

No. Not a good way to start the day.

"I see you got the word on the new partner assignments announced today, Tyler." Thankfully, Sam found a pen in his inside suit pocket and smiled as he pulled it out, clicking loudly before he started making notes on a small notepad. Not looking at Kate, he said, "We got this," and started to walk towards an open window near the entry door to the kitchen. He noticed John following him out of the corner of his eye. A flurry of activity also told him that Kate was right behind him, on his six.

"Oh no you don't! You heard what the Captain said! We're partners. Well, until they get my transfer papers processed, that is," Kate rapidly explained as she hurried to keep up with Sam.

Ignoring her, well, TRYING to ignore her, Sam approached the open window, stood back and noticed some dark smudges around the window lock. He kneeled down in front of it and saw the tell-tale scratches near the lock. Standing up, he almost knocked Kate over in his haste to wave over one of the crime scene specialists.

Biting back a grimace at the quick and unexpected contact with Kate, he ground out, "Don't you have a suspect to torture or something?"

"Hey, those charges were never substantiated," she answered quickly, reaching into her backpack and pulling out a digital camera.

Sam directed the CSI tech who approached him, "Make sure you take photos of this before you print the entire area," he explained as he pointed to the scratch marks and smudges near the window. He heard the lunch lady's shrill voice again in the background and turned back to Kate. "Look. You want to help me solve this case?"

"I'm not going to HELP you do anything, Sam. I'LL solve this case," she said as she snapped a few photos of the lock.

"Fine. Stop playing Annie Lebowitz and go over and talk to 'Lunch Lady Mildred.' She seems a tad bit unnerved over losing a few gallons of school cafeteria ice cream." Sam could feel Kate's glare as he walked away from her.

Screw it. Sometimes wishes DO come true. He thought he saw a custodian out in the hallway with a pack of cigarettes sticking out of his shirt pocket.

The more things change, the more they stay the same. Guess that means Sam's still mad at me. She wasn't about to let him have the last word and started to follow him, but abruptly stopped when she saw him talking to a janitor and bumming a cigarette from him.

"Interesting. I really DO get under his skin," Kate muttered as she turned back towards the cafeteria. Her handheld radio vibrated, alerting her to an incoming message, effectively breaking her concentration on Sam and his obvious return to smoking.

"Unit 2370, Code 10-90 at Fifth Third Bank, Fountain Square Location. You copy?" Excitement ran through Kate as she heard the radio dispatcher notify her of a possible bank robbery in progress. Turning the volume down on her radio slightly, so as to not alarm any of the civilians still on the scene, she turned to face the door and replied, "Unit 2370, 10-4."

Kate quickly located John, who was taking a witness statement from one of the cafeteria workers. She waved him over, "You're going to have to finish up here and make sure you talk to Mildred. Get her down to the station and take her statement there. Sam and I got another call." Kate fished her small notebook from her jacket pocket and quickly wrote down the time of the call and the location of the bank. She stopped writing to look at John, who had grown quiet and just stood there, obviously waiting for her to finish her thought.

"Bank alarm tripped at the Fifth-Third on Fountain Square." Kate keyed her radio to alert Sam of an incoming transmission.

"Downtown bank robbery? This early in the morning? That doesn't seem, right. Bank's closed. Usually downtown banks are hit during lunch hour or later in the day," John said making some notes in his notebook.

"Yeah. I know. I also heard some radio transmission earlier that two gun shops got hit about an hour ago, one in Deer Park and one in Bond Hill." Kate held her hand up to John and said into her radio, "Unit 1979, we have a 10-89 on Fountain Square. You copy?" She didn't wait for Sam to respond, but said to John, "We're out of here. Call if you need anything." Kate turned and walked towards the door just when her radio squawked, "Unit 2370, 10-4." Her cell phone rang, and she answered it, seeing it was Sam calling her.

"I'll meet you there. I don't want to leave my car here," Sam shouted as Kate double-timed it out of the school.

"Affirmative," Kate answered as she ran towards her unmarked Toyota. Shoving her notebook and cell phone back in her pocket, she grabbed her keys and unlocked the car with her remote. She got in, tossing her radio on the passenger seat and grabbed the light from under the same seat and stuck it on her dashboard. Turning on the ignition and activating the lights and sirens, she felt the same thrill of excitement she always did whenever she answered a call. "I don't care if Sam is pissed at me about the McHenry case. I STILL love this job," she muttered to herself as she picked up the radio and keyed the dispatcher, "Unit 2370, 10-76," repeating the police code to confirm she was en route to the bank. Two calls in two hours and it wasn't even a full moon, she thought, as she weaved in and out of traffic.

Kate stole a look at the clock on her dashboard, noticing that it was just now turning 0800 hours. It had been a full morning already. As she was making her way downtown towards the bank alarm, the radio traffic coming out of the dispatcher's office seemed unnaturally heavy this morning. Oh, sure, weekdays always seemed to have more calls for service for the police officers, in terms of traffic accidents due to the morning drive time, but many of the calls today were for detectives, which was very unusual this time of day.

Kate was still about a mile away from the bank when her cell phone rang.

Seeing it was Sam calling, she answered, "Yeah."

"How far out are you?" Sam barked into the phone.

"Three blocks. I'll be there in a sec."

"The unis already cleared the building. No one is in there." Sam's voice crackled a bit over the mobile phone.

"Sam, I'm disconnecting. I just arrived on scene." With that she put the phone back in her pocket. Just as she pulled up outside of the bank in the center of downtown Cincinnati, Kate heard another call for an alarm tripped at the Federal Building. Flipping off her siren, but keeping her light flashing, she turned off her car, locked it, and saw Sam had already beat her there. The way he drove, no wonder. He didn't really drive, but rather put the car in "F" for fly. Kate had been accused of being an erratic driver over the years, but she had nothing on Sam. Even her dad, a retired police chief, agreed with her on that.

She walked over to where Sam stood and saw him popping some gum into his mouth. Kate tried to hide a smile when she realized it was nicotine gum. Sam looked at her and growled, "Not one word." His jaw furiously worked the gum and Kate saw him seemingly relax a tiny bit as the nicotine hit his bloodstream. It really pissed her off that even though he seemed to despise her, she liked him. A lot. He was a good cop. And so freaking good looking that it sometimes hurt to look at him. She would rather have bamboo shoots shoved under her fingernails before she ever admitted that to anyone, though. She'd never hear the end of that, to be sure. Get a grip on yourself, girl, she thought to herself as she stumbled while thinking of a snappy comeback for her nemesis.

"Hey, it's not my business, if you've got to feed that monkey on your back," she replied as she pulled a pair of latex gloves out of her pocket and snapped them on. She saw the Duty Officer, Captain Wilkes, already on site conferring with the two uniformed cops who'd answered the call and cleared the building. She jerked her head towards the Duty Officer and walked towards him.

"More like a gorilla," he muttered to himself as he followed her, putting on a pair of latex gloves.

"What's the situation, Captain?" Kate asked as she nodded hello to the two uniformed cops. She pulled out her notebook and turned to a fresh page.

"Wyatt, Tyler," the Captain said by way of hello. "Apparent break-in. Adams and Clark arrived on scene twenty minutes ago to answer a tripped alarm and saw evidence of an illegal entry. The bank manager's been called and is on her way in to open the vaults for inspection."

Kate was about to speak when Captain Wilkes' radio started squawking and he held up his hand for Kate to wait a minute. Kate turned away from the Captain and motioned to Sam to step away from him for a second. "Don't you find all this rather strange?" she asked Sam. He surprised her by not arguing with her.

"I was thinking the same thing on the way down here from the school." He jotted down a few notes in his pad and checked his watch.

"Seriously, Sam. Since when do TWO gun shops get hit within an hour of one another? This isn't Dodge City. Gun shops in Cincinnati don't typically get hit. And now an alarm tripped at a downtown bank AND the Federal Building?" Kate shook her head in disbelief.

"I agree. It's almost as if..." Sam's voice wandered off.

A tickle of fear tiptoed down Kate's spine as she looked at Sam's face. Not knowing why she felt so apprehensive, her mouth felt like cotton was jammed in it, making it difficult for her to talk.

"What, Sam? What is it?"

It was one of those weird moments of clarity that washed over a person, every so often in life, and Sam was smack dab in the middle of one at that very instant. The wispy niggles of fear currently tap-dancing down his spine were at war with the normally solid base of rational thinking that Sam was proud of, and known for, every day he was on the job. And somewhere in the back of his mind was his partner's voice asking him over and over, "What, Sam? What is it?"

Sam motioned Kate over to the corner of the room, out of the path of any security cameras and away from anyone who might overhear their conversation. He whispered into her ear, "Did you notice that metallic odor coming from the vault door?" He jerked his head in the direction of the bank vault, which was covered with a wrought iron, gated door, in the dead center of the room.

Kate slightly nodded her head in agreement and whispered, "Yeah, now that you mention it." She looked at the two uniformed cops standing closer to the front door of the bank, talking with Captain Wilkes, and then looked back at Sam. "What is it? Is there any danger?"

Sam replied, "No, I don't think so. But that metallic smell reminds me of Semtex."

"Semtex? What?" Kate looked at him with a questioning glare. Sam nodded his head in the affirmative.

Kate shook her head again, in disagreement. "No. Plastic explosives don't have any smell to them. They're virtually impossible to discover. Man, what is with you? You should know that. Maybe you SHOULD keep smoking, because you're not thinking clearly at all." Kate moved to walk away from him.

Sam grabbed her arm. "You're right. Most plastics DON'T have any scent to them. But, there's some construction grade explosives that have a chemical compound added to them to alert crews to their use on demolition sites." Sam's chilling explanation stopped Kate dead in her tracks. She turned back to him.

"And?" She asked, obviously waiting for an explanation.

"And, the Feds issued a BOLO late yesterday on a guy who liked to knock off banks." Sam looked at his watch and pulled his radio out of his jacket pocket. Keying the radio, he quietly spoke into the device, "Dispatch, Unit 1789 requests transfer to Desk Sergeant on Duty."

"Yeah? So? Lots of bad guys like to rob banks. And they're all doing time, courtesy of the State of Ohio." Kate made a note in her small notebook and looked at Sam when she was finished, "I don't see the connection."

Opening her mouth to say something else, the radio crackled to life just at that moment. "Unit 1789, Sergeant

Boothe asked that you call him on your mobile phone. Over." Momentarily annoyed, Sam replied, "Unit 1789. Copy that."

"What's up? Why are you calling him?" Kate popped a breath mint into her mouth, glaring at Sam a little.

Sam ignored her and unclipped his mobile phone from his waistband. He hit the speed dial for the desk sergeant on duty for the day. Watching Kate, he remembered how addicted she was to those mints, constantly sucking them down during the course of the day.

He activated the speakerphone and motioned for Kate to move closer to the phone. Once the sergeant answered, Sam asked him to read the 'Be On the Look Out' notice he'd previously read about the bank robber. As the desk sergeant read the quick notice from the FBI, both Sam and Kate frowned at the similarities of the bank robberies that the FBI issued just yesterday, to today's crime scene at the bank.

The partners looked at one another and both mouthed the same word at the same time, "Semtex."

Not wanting to draw any attention to them, or get the rumor mill cranking back at the police station by having the uniformed cops overhear them, Sam took the phone off of speaker and thanked the sergeant for the information and quickly disconnected the call. "Let's get the CSI unit in here to dust for prints and see what else pops up," Sam said to Kate as he turned towards the front of the bank.

Waving over Captain Wyatt, he brought him up to speed on what he wanted to do. The captain quickly nodded his agreement and radioed to the dispatcher to see how close the crime scene unit was to the bank. "Listen. Homeland Security wants me over at the Federal Building as their local liaison while the crime scene is processed for evidence. Do you both have what you need for right now?" The captain waited until both Sam and Kate nodded their agreement before he left for the three-block walk to the newer crime scene.

"Hey Sam, the techs are here. I'll give them a quick status update on what to process on the scene, OK?" Kate asked as she watched one of the uniformed cops opening the door for their technicians.

"Great," Sam replied. He noticed a scrap of paper sticking out from under the vault door and walked over to it. Bending down to look at it, he realized it was larger than a scrap sized piece of paper. It was a torn sheet of paper that looked like a computer printout of some kind. Not wanting to touch it, he called, "Kate! Got something! Bring the camera!"

He heard his partner relay the message to one of the newly arrived technicians and stood up to give them some room. Kate started snapping shots of the paper from several different angles and the technician, Alice, one of the departments' more senior crime scene investigators, put down her instrument case and opened the lid. She pulled out a small ruler to lay next to the paper to give it some scale in the photograph. Alice had a large digital camera hanging on a strap around her neck and began snapping a few photos from various angles. Sam smiled as he watched her. He'd worked more crime scenes than he could remember with Alice. He liked her thoroughness in working the scenes.

Sam squatted down next to her and peered closely at the paper. He looked at Alice and then back at the paper and then back to Alice.

He rocked back on his feet and scratched the top of his head. "Is that what I think it is?" letting out a derisive bark of laughter.

Alice smiled as she pulled out a pair of long tongs from her instrument case. "Yep. I do believe so." She looked at Sam and asked, "OK if I pick this up?" He nodded and watched her pick up the torn sheet of paper from the floor.

Kate snapped a few more photos of the sheet of paper as Alice held it in the tongs. Sam put his hand under Alice's gloved hand and moved it up about a foot so he could read it. Kate moved closer to the both of them and Alice held it so they could both read it.

Alice's hand started shaking a little and both Sam and Kate looked at her and smiled at the same time when they realized she was laughing.

The paper shook harder as Alice was on the verge of laughing hysterically. Even Sam felt his mood lighten just the tiniest bit as he realized what he was looking at.

Still chuckling, Alice pulled a paper bag out of her tool box and snapped it open. Carefully placing the paper inside the bag, so as to not bend it, she sealed the bag with red tape and initialed it to maintain the chain of evidence.

Sam and Kate watched Alice as she pulled out her evidence log to make a notation about the paper. They smiled at one another as Alice laughed, "Never fails to amaze me just how dumb the bad guys really are!"

Clark, the younger of the two uniformed cops, walked up to them and seeing Sam, Kate and Alice smiling, asked, "What'd ya find?"

Sam laughed as he explained, "You won't even believe it. Hell, I don't believe it, but as soon as we get the cyber-crimes guys to verify it, I think we've just uncovered a homegrown crime plot."

Kate kept jotting down notes in her small flip notebook as Sam explained to Clark, "We found a torn sheet of paper that was actually an email from one of the bad guys to his dumb ass partner in crime!" His radio squawked at that moment and he answered it.

Kate jumped in and explained, on behalf of Sam, "From what we could see, these guys are planning on moving a load of plastic explosives out of state to give to a gang in exchange for drugs, weapons and ammo! What a bunch of idiots!"

Clark looked dumbstruck and replied, "Seriously? You're not just trying to haze the junior cop on the scene? Because, umm, so, yeah, I've already had that fun experience this month."

Alice looked up from her log book and laughed. "You're THAT Clark?" She snorted. "Hell, son. Even I heard about that one. How long did it take you to figure out that your expert witness also thinks he's Obi Wan Kenobi from *Star Wars*?"

Sam walked back, holding his now silent radio. "You're never going to believe this. Remember good ol' lunch lady

Mildred?" He shoved his radio into his jacket pocket and patted his front pocket as if feeling for a phantom pack of cigarettes. Realizing what he was doing, he laughed to himself and looked up at his partner, Alice and Clark.

Kate let out a deep sigh and waved her hand in front of him and said, "Yeaaahhh?"

"John Quinn just called to say the lunch lady gave it up." He laughed as he remembered watching her earlier this morning. Yeegads, was that really only four hours ago? he asked himself.

"What? Mildred?" Kate asked. Alice and Clark had no idea what he was talking about. Sam quickly told them about the break-in at the school earlier this morning and how the only thing that appeared to be taken was ice cream.

Sam finished explaining what Mildred told them. "Evidently these same morons who had tried to mastermind a huge heist involving a weapons swap for Semtex with a gang in Chicago also thought to steal an industrial sized freezer full of ice cream meant for school kids." Sam made a few notes in his pad before telling Alice he and Kate would see her back at the lab towards the end of their shift.

"Where are we going?" Kate asked Sam as he motioned for her to follow him.

"You and I are going down to the cybercrimes unit to get warrants on the computers involved in the email message we found on the floor back there. Then, we're going to pick up Mildred's dumb shit grandsons." He walked quickly towards the front door but stopped when he heard Clark shout

out to him, "Hey! What about me?"

Sam laughed when he turned around in time to see Alice jab the young police officer in the shoulder, "Didn't you hear the news, Obi Wan? You're going to help me process the rest of this crime scene!" Yeah. Just what a junior grade uniformed cop wanted to do. Work as a CSI's assistant at a crime scene.

Sam was still laughing when he met Kate at the front door to the bank. She smiled at him, popping yet another breath mint into her mouth. "You know, we dodged a bullet on this one, don'tcha?" she asked as she nodded her head in the direction of the bank vault.

Turning serious for a moment, he looked her in the eye and said, "Yeah. I know. Who would have thought our criminals would have been turned in by their own grandmother? They really pissed her off when they stole the ice cream, huh?" He waited for her to walk through the door and followed her.

Kate almost pocketed her mints, but hesitated for a moment before offering them to Sam. "You might want to try these. They'll make you smell better than cigarettes ever did."

Sam almost refused, but smiled at her before accepting one. "Everybody's a critic these days," he muttered before they both walked to their cars.

"You can be grumpy if you want to, Sam, but we've got some bad guys to pick up," she said in a sing-song voice.

"Yeah. And once we're done, let's stop by the Pitty-Pat Cafe. I'm suddenly hungry for some ice cream."

Time's Tempest: The Storm
Jennette Marie Powell

Rex woke to white. Where the hell was he? Crisp sheet beneath his clammy hands. White walls. White ceiling. Three brass-railed beds in a row beside the one he lay in. Hospital? No, not with that old-fashioned, lift-open, wooden window across from him, with a telephone pole outside. A telephone pole with the number 140 spray-painted in orange on it. He remembered seeing it while he was cutting up the tree that had fallen in the backyard of that old house in Dayton they said was a research agency—

Holy fuck, was he one of their experiments?

A metallic taste flooded his mouth.

Then he remembered. A little boy had come tearing out from behind the garage, made Rex drop the chainsaw. He'd cut his leg, bad... he could still hear the saw's buzz, still smell his own blood, as he'd realized he was going to die...

But there he was, inside the house, judging from the telephone pole. And he was warm, like he'd just woke from a sound sleep, could almost feel the blood coursing through the leg he thought he'd cut off.

The bed creaked as he pushed himself up—or tried. Had they drugged him?

"Hey!" a girl's voice drifted from down a hallway. "Hellooooo?" Her ruffled, black dress swooshed as she flounced into the room. "Hi, I'm Taylor," she said in a too-loud voice.

About twenty, new at... whatever. "No BS," Rex said. "What the hell's going on here?"

"Welcome to the Saturn Society. You uh, had an accident with your chainsaw."

"Yeah, I remember that." He looked down at his leg, though the sheet covered it.

He should have bled out. He should be dead. "What the hell—"

"You died." Taylor pronounced the words carefully, slowly, as if she thought he was an idiot or didn't understand English. "You're one of us now. A time-traveler."

Rex scowled as he gazed out over Lake Erie, the leaden gray skies and choppy waters mocking him.

This was not what his first trip back in time was supposed to be.

The wind smacked his starched, white shirtsleeves against his arms like rubber bands. Tony had told him that he should research, find out exactly what had happened in Put-In-Bay that day, pick the exact year he wanted to go back to. But no, Rex was spontaneous, he didn't do that shit. He lived for the moment, always had. So he'd said, what the hell, he'd always liked Ohio's "Little Key West." He figured he'd go back to 1916, before the U.S. got involved in World War I, but after Perry's Memorial was built, so he'd have that to use as a touchpoint for time travel. So he'd simply pictured the giant Greek column tower, just like it was in his time; imagined the slightly-fishy smell of the lake, pretended there was a giant waterslide, built on a rickety-looking wooden roller coaster frame, like he'd seen in a photo in his great-grandma's stuff. He'd pictured the pier leading out to it, felt the grass in the park beneath his bare feet warmed by the sun, heard the laughter of kids playing, their shouts as they shot down the slide.

It had been that way when he'd arrived three days ago, before he'd had to check into a hotel, and sleep off the effects of time travel, as Taylor had warned him he'd need to do.

He'd imagined the sound of the all-female brass sextet Great-grandma had talked about, that played every summer in the park by the monument. Imagined the taste of the fresh roasted peanuts the man sold from the cart on the pier—the cart which was now covered with a tarp and chained to a little wooden building with a sign that read Bathing Suit Rentals–Snacks, in anticipation of the coming storm.

He squeezed the handful of change in his pocket. The park and the beach were deserted. The Bathing Suite Rentals–Snacks shop was battened down. Anyone with any sense had left with the storm coming in. The band was long gone. The streetcar had departed a good ten minutes ago for the Hotel Victory on the far end of the island. The driver had shouted "last call!" and had given Rex a weird look when he shook his head.

But something had made him stay at the beach, gazing out over Lake Erie at the deserted waterslide, mainland Ohio now obscured by the oncoming storm.

Thunder rumbled, and his sense of gloom deepened.

He'd never find Gretchen before that Pull thing yanked him back to the present, and she'd die... again.

His head jerked. Who the hell was Gretchen?

He stared across the graying beach, unseeing, waiting for more info from whatever had prompted that thought—it was like a voice in his head, but it was okay, it was his own. But now the voice was silent.

Wind buffeted him, riffling his short hair. Had the waves grown higher in the ten minutes he'd stood there?

Rex's gaze narrowed. A ways down the shore, a pair of sailboats bobbed against a private dock, their sails furled tight. No one was stupid enough to be at the beach now. If Gretchen—whoever the hell she was—was out in that, she was most likely already dead.

As he turned to walk toward the village—maybe he'd wait out the storm at the Round House with a beer and a bite to eat—a piece of paper slapped him in the face, carried by the wind.

He peeled it off his cheek, and held it in front of him with two hands, as if it were a scroll. The wind tried to take it, but Rex's grip was stronger—for now.

The North Shore Sextet, it read across the top, above a grainy photo of the band. Six women in long, white, high-waisted dresses held musical instruments, and sat in a ring around a smiling, tuxedo-clad man. Rex's lips tightened. Couldn't blame the guy for smiling, those ladies were hot—

Then he noticed the names beside each of the girls. Theresa Wilson played the tuba. Claire McKinley played trumpet. And the saxophone player beside her, with the sparkling eyes and blond hair with one chunk that escaped her up-do—Rex bit his lip. Gretchen Schwartz.

Waterslide. Something—he didn't know what—compelled him, and he moved toward the shore.

Are you nuts? Beneath the constant howl of the wind, something banged—a loose board somewhere nearby, maybe.

He stopped. The rickety-looking, wooden structure in the lake shuddered in the wind. What the hell was he thinking?

Gretchen.

Rex looked down at his fist, and slowly opened it. The wind snatched the musicians' flyer from it, and the piece of paper disappeared before he could see where it went—

Waterslide.

That strange compulsion again. "What the hell," he muttered as he trudged across the grassy area toward the pier.

The wind tore at his shirt, filling his mouth with the taste of dirt before he thought to shut it. He gazed up and down the deserted beach, and out across the frothy waves.

Wherever Gretchen was, she wasn't out there.

Spitting to get the grit out of his mouth, Rex walked along the long, wooden building, which a sign identified as a bathhouse, the wind practically blowing him to the other end. A big gust swirled down the hill from the monument, making him stumble on the gravel walkway. As he righted himself, something black wedged against the building's foundation caught his eye.

A woman's lace-up, high-heel ankle boot. He picked it up. The wind gusted again, and he braced a hand against the bathhouse corner as he turned the shoe over in his other hand. Shiny and new-looking, not something that blew out of the trash. Someone had paid a lot of money for that shoe.

He gazed at the village in the distance, beyond the monument. Wouldn't hurt to turn it in, a good deed he could do to buy his way into heaven.

The banging sound he'd heard before came again, and this time, he spotted its source. On the waterslide, a section of the lattice that lined the walkway had come loose, and was banging in the wind—

"No..." The wind stole the rest of Rex's words, his throat dry.

At the far end of the lattice-lined section lay the mate to the shoe he held in his hand. And wearing that shoe lay a woman in a long, white dress, nearly hidden by the lattice.

Rex's throat felt full of sand as he raced into the wind down the pier. Fat, cold raindrops smacked his face. The lattice banged again, harder, and Rex thought he saw the waterslide shudder, as if for emphasis.

Finally he reached the woman and knelt beside her. She lay on her side, her face covered by wavy, water-darkened curls that had escaped her up-do. Dirt smudged her dress, and the wind had pushed her skirt halfway up her legs, revealing torn, once-white stockings.

"Hey!" Rex shook her shoulder. Warm, thank God.

But she didn't stir. Damn. He dug into his pocket for his cell phone before he remembered he'd left it at the campground at the far end of the island, in the twenty-first century. "Dumbass," he muttered. There'd be no 9-1-1 either, even if he had a phone to call with, not to mention any service.

He had to get her out of there before the storm hit in full force.

As if to emphasize his thoughts, the sparse patter of rain on the lake grew into a steady roar.

Gently, he turned the woman over. Wind and rain buffeted the waterslide, shaking its flimsy frame as he got his first look at her face.

Gretchen. Why wasn't he surprised?

He shook her shoulder once more—"Gretchen! Wake up!"—but she didn't move. Lightning split the sky, and thunder boomed.

He had to get her to shelter, any shelter.

Only one thing he could do. "Okay, let's go." He scooped the unconscious musician off the pier and draped her over his shoulder, grateful for his strength honed by years of physical labor, cutting down trees, and splitting wood by hand.

Squinting to keep the rain out of his eyes as much as he could, he trudged toward the monument through the deluge, which plastered his already-sodden clothes to his body. The nearest shelter was the Bathing Suit Rentals–Snacks shack. The white, wooden structure sported a decent paint job, although between gusts of rain he could see where the corner had been scuffed off to display numerous other colors of paint.

It had been there a long time, and would probably be their best bet to ride out the storm. Wind rocked the waterslide, making the wood creak and shudder, affirming his decision.

Finally, he made it to the clothing and snack shop and climbed the slatted wooden steps. He peered at the door. A silver padlock hung from a metal loop. "Shit." Why hadn't he thought about that? Of course it would be locked.

But he was Rex the Chainsaw Guy, and Rex the Chainsaw Guy didn't let a little thing like a padlock stop him.

That was more easily dealt with when he had his truck and tools with him. But he didn't exactly carry his bolt cutter around otherwise. Luckily, he never went anywhere without his Swiss Army knife and lighter.

He patted Gretchen's back. "Honey, I'm going to have to put you down." He lowered her to the steps, along with the shoe he still carried, then stepped up beside her to get at that lock.

Just a typical, flat piece of metal with a slot, latched over a loop. Both were bolted to the wood with ordinary, metal screws. Enough to discourage the casual thief, but not someone as determined as Rex. He dug out his knife, flipped up the flathead screwdriver, and set to work. A few minutes later, he yanked the door open (almost whacking Gretchen's head), picked her and her shoe up, and carried them inside.

The floor was half filled with boxes and crates—food and drink, he hoped—leaving an empty spot on the floor maybe four by eight feet. Racks of clothing that felt like long pajamas, but Rex realized were early twentieth century swimsuits, stretched across the building beneath the rafters.

He laid Gretchen on the wooden floor. Rain and wind lashed the building's back wall as he moved to inspect the crates. She'd need something to drink if she came to.

The nearest crate was labeled Spun-Rite Fairy Floss Sugar, Blue. He remembered hearing the Aussies calling cotton candy that, one time when a charity group had a carnival for the soldiers in the Sandbox. Well, that would be disgustingly sweet without being made into cotton candy, but he and Gretchen could eat it if they got desperate.

The next crate was labeled Swifty-Pop Popcorn. Not very useful unpopped. He moved on. Health Kup, 8 oz., read the next box. What the hell was a Health Kup? Then he took a closer look at the carton and saw a small line drawing, along with the name The Individual Drinking Cup Company. "Rex, you dumbass," he muttered. But drinking cups were good, because cups meant beverages. He grabbed the box and put it on the floor beside him, then grabbed the one under it and the next. As he bent to grab the bottom one, a soft moan came from behind him, barely audible over the rain pounding the shed.

Rex leaped to Gretchen, almost knocking over a crate, and crouched beside her. "Hey!"

Her head lolled to one side and her mouth opened, but nothing came out.

Rex touched her shoulder. Her eyelids fluttered. "Gretchen?"

Her eyes opened—pale blue, he could barely see by the scant light coming in around the boarded-up service window. She tried to speak, but only air came out.

Rex patted her shoulder. "Shh, it's okay." She moved her mouth again, but only a dry gasp came out. Probably dehydrated. Her gaze darted to the back wall, where the rain and wind pummeled the shack. Rex spoke in what he hoped was a reassuring tone of voice. "I think we're safe for now, but I need to find you something to drink."

"Uhhh," she whispered.

Rex stood. "I'm gonna get you some water... I think there's some back there somewhere, okay?"

"Uhhh," she repeated, tipping her chin down.

Rex took that as a yes and moved back to the crates. After he moved two more stacks of boxes, he finally caught a glimpse of the front corner—and a water cooler, much like those found in twenty-first century offices. The glass jug was half full, and when he turned the tap on the white porcelain base, water came out. "Hot damn!"

Luckily, cups were in no short supply—he'd moved three boxes full, so he tore into one, and was soon back at Gretchen's side.

Her eyes darted nervously from side to side, at Rex, and aside again. "Wha...?" she managed.

Rex held up the cup and sat beside her. "Can you sit up?"

She allowed him to help her, wincing as she moved. He lifted the cup to her lips.

She drank, hesitantly at first, then in big gulps, until the cup was empty. "More?" Rex asked.

She wiped her mouth with the back of her hand and shook her head once. "Thank... you," she said breathily.

"You're wel—"

Something slammed against the shack's back wall, shaking the building.

Gretchen's gaze darted around the tiny room. "Where... am I?"

Rex sat beside her. "Well, I found you passed out on that big waterslide. That noise was probably something from there—it didn't seem too stable. That's why I brought you here—the little building where they rent out swimsuits and sell snacks."

"Little building where...? Wha...?"

"By the waterslide, near Perry's Memorial—"

"I know." Her voice was growing stronger. "But how..."

"What happened to you?" Rex guessed she probably didn't know how she wound up on the waterslide, but if she had a concussion, wasn't he supposed to keep her awake and talking?

"I don't... know." She leaned back against a crate, and a shuddering breath escaped her. An urge to pull her into his arms struck Rex, but he feared that would only scare her. For all she knew, he could have been the guy who did... whatever... to her, knocked her out, and left her out in the storm.

Her blue eyes fixed on his face. "You... I've..." She clamped her mouth shut, as if she'd started to say something she shouldn't, and a strange expression flitted across her face.

"Who... are you?"

"My name's Rex. They call me Rex the Chainsaw Guy because that's what I do, cut down trees and stuff. I didn't come here for that, but I bet there'll be plenty of work for me once this storm's over. Except I don't have my chainsaw..." Realizing he was blathering like a dumbass, he stopped. Had chainsaws even been invented yet?

"You speak... strangely," she said. "You aren't from around here, are you?"

"Uh..." Rex peered up at the rafters, trying to clear his head. Taylor and Tony had both told him it was important not to tell about the Society, especially because in some time periods, being able to disappear by time traveling was a crime, or could at least get you in trouble. "I'm uh, from Dayton." Hey, it was the truth.

She looked down with a nod, twiddling her fingers. Shaky fingers.

"So what happened to you? How'd you end up on the waterslide—I mean, what's the last thing you remember?"

She looked down and picked at her thumbnail. "We were down at Fox's dock, waiting for the steamship to leave for Toledo. The band, I mean. I don't know how long you've been here, but—"

"The North Shore Sextet," Rex said. She looked up. "I uh, wasn't here in time to see a show, but I saw the flyers. You're Gretchen Schwartz, the saxophone player."

"Ye-es," she said carefully.

"I don't forget a pretty face." Rex clamped his mouth

shut. He shouldn't have said that, now she'd think he was coming on to her.

Except he couldn't exactly tell her about the voice in his head. Better she think him a pig than crazy. Although people accused him of that all the time, too. Better get back to business. "So you were waiting for the steamship...?" Rex had seen the gigantic steamers carrying hundreds of passengers to and from the islands—a far cry from the ferry he'd ridden over on in the twenty-first century.

"I was running late," she said. "I'd gotten drawn into a conversation with an old woman on the streetcar, so everyone else was already on the steamer. There was this gentleman loitering behind the shipping house... I'd seen him on the streetcar, there was something about him... he didn't look quite right."

She shivered, and Rex wondered if it was from the memory, or because it was getting cooler in the drafty shack. He wanted to scoot over beside her, slip his arm around her—to warm her up, nothing more—but that wouldn't be a good idea. "So what about this guy wasn't right?"

"He looked angry. Not at anything specific, just in general. At everything." She met Rex's gaze, and though he couldn't see much in the dim light, he could sense her fear—not of him, not of the storm, but of the angry man. "And his clothing. It looked... like it was years out of style, yet I couldn't identify how old it might be. He looked like he was looking for someone. And then he saw me, right after I noticed. And he looked even angrier. After that, he stopped looking around, just kept staring at me."

"Weird." Could the guy be a time traveler? Then Rex dismissed the idea. What were the odds? "Maybe he thought you were hot, and was cranky because he knew he didn't have a chance—"

Gretchen wrinkled her nose. "Hot? I don't think so, the weather was quite pleasant."

"I mean good-looking." Shit, he'd screwed up, used modern slang. He hoped she'd think it was something people said in Dayton.

"No, because later..." She gazed off to the side.

"What?"

"I'm trying to remember... at the dock..." She reached for the water cup with a shaking hand.

"You want another drink?" At her nod, Rex grabbed the cup and refilled it. But when he handed it to her, she didn't lift it to her mouth.

"He cornered me." She spoke barely above a whisper. "He said... I had something that belonged to him, and he wanted it back. I told him he must be mistaken, but he was quite insistent. Then..." Her chin lowered as she swallowed. She lifted the cup to her mouth and took a sip. "He called me a 'high-class broad' and said I shouldn't be with those shady musicians. That I needed to go with him." She took another drink. "I told him I was sorry, but I had to go. That's when he grabbed my arms and dragged me away. I screamed, but..."

She licked her lip, and the sight sent a jolt right to Rex's groin. Not happening, he told himself. "No one heard?"

She shook her head. "The steamer was about to leave, so no one was nearby. All the dock hands were busy, and then the ship blew her horn..."

She lifted the cup to her mouth again, shaking so hard she would have spilled water, if she hadn't already drained the cup. Rex started to move over, then hesitated. "Are you cold?"

She met his gaze, and the fear in her eyes tugged at him. "It is a bit chilly in here."

"Would it be okay if I sit beside you? 'Cause I'm a little cold, too." He threw that in on a whim, hoping it would put her more at ease with him, if not the situation.

She managed a shaky nod, so Rex scooted across the gritty floorboards until he sat beside her—near enough to feel the warmth radiating from her side, but not touching. Maybe it was his imagination, but he thought she shivered a little less. "What did the guy do when you screamed?"

"He said that's not going to help you, Miss Sch—" She gasped and lifted her fingers to her lips. "I'd almost forgotten. He knew my name!"

"But you didn't know him?"

She shook her head.

Getting stronger, Rex was glad to see. "Maybe he just recognized you from the flyer, like I did." Except when he thought about it, Rex realized he really hadn't. He'd known who she was, even though he'd never seen her before.

Could it have something to do with the time travel?

That didn't matter now. "What else?" Rex said.

She gazed at the floor, brows pressed down. "Something smelled strange... not like a man's cologne, but sweet... and then... Next I knew, I was here. With you."

Rex's jaw clamped shut. The guy had drugged her, then left her on the rickety waterslide as a storm was coming in, probably to die. But why? "You're sure you didn't know the guy?"

"Positive. I'd remember that face if I'd seen it before." She shuddered and crossed her arms over her chest, rubbing her hands over her upper arms. "He would have been a nice-looking fellow, had he not been so... so..."

"Creepy?"

"Yes."

The rain lashed the shack's back wall harder, as if to emphasize her point.

He would have to keep an eye out for the guy when the storm was over.

She stared across the cramped room, though Rex doubted she was studying the plain, whitewashed boards.

Rex let his gaze drift over her curling hair that hung in ringlets where it had come loose, giving it a sexy, bedhead look. He studied her graceful neck, her round, smooth breasts straining against the fabric of her dress. Her slender, long fingers that made him want to hear her play the saxophone—then see how she'd play him.

He stared down at his left hand, resting on the floor, inches away from her hip. He itched to slide it around her narrow shoulders. As much as he'd like to get busy with this woman, his lustful self would have to stay in the backseat. Right now, his honorable side was in charge.

Better get his mind off what he couldn't have. He held up the ankle boot he'd found near the bathhouse. "Uh, I found your other shoe."

"Oh! Why, thank you. I'm afraid I spent more than I should have on these, but I just had to have them, and..." she trailed off as he grabbed her foot—soft, delicate thing—and slid it into the ankle boot, feeling like a prince who'd just found his own sopping, wet Cinderella. "Thank you," she repeated in a whisper as he pulled the laces and tied them in a bow.

"My pleasure." And it was. But what the hell had possessed him to put her shoe on? If he'd tried that in his own time, chances were, he'd have gotten slapped, yet Gretchen didn't seem to mind.

She shifted beside him, bracing her hands on the floor as she pushed herself up with a grimace. She wobbled, then steadied. "You okay?" Rex asked.

Her mouth pressed into a line, she gave a nod, then took a hesitant step toward the door.

"I don't think you want—" Rex began.

She pushed the door open, and the wind stole it, slamming it against the outside of the shack. "Good heavens!"

She leaned out and reached for the handle, as the wind rocked the shack. Rex leaped to her side and caught her around the waist, just as she stumbled and nearly fell down the steps.

He yanked her inside, pulling her against him.

"Oh!" She found her footing, and even though he didn't want to, he released her.

She swiped a hand over her face to wipe the water off. "Thank you."

"I tried to tell you." Rex slicked his hair back, raining more water onto the floor. He squeezed more out of his shirt, then sat on the floor in his earlier spot, leaning against the back wall.

Gretchen sat beside him, close enough that the water dripping from her hair fell on his elbow. "We could be here a while, I'm afraid."

"Uh... yeah." Rex stared at the floor. What little light there was in the cramped shack was fading. Night was falling, yet the storm showed no sign of letting up.

He doubted he'd be able to sleep, between the rain pounding on the building, and his stomach, which was starting to rumble. Not to mention Gretchen's nearness.

What a screwed-up situation, trapped in an isolated shack, alone with a hot woman. One his damned sense of honor wouldn't let him even think about touching.

So he talked. He asked her questions, learned the band was from Toledo, and they were just starting to build a following there and in Detroit. "The weather forecasters are saying this could be the storm of the century," Gretchen said.

Rex doubted it, but he kept that to himself.

"Mary and Theresa wanted to cancel and leave the island early, but Ritchie—he's our band leader—he insisted that we play our last gig, and that we could be home before the storm hit."

"I'm sure they made it," Rex said. He couldn't help but wonder if there were more to it. Maybe Ritchie knew the creepy dude in the outdated clothes, had planned to meet up, and hand Gretchen over to him—

Oh, come on, don't be stupid. Rex was seeing connections that weren't there.

Thunder boomed, and Gretchen fidgeted beside him. He tried to get her mind off the situation. "So how'd you get into music?"

They talked for hours, it seemed. Before long, she started asking him questions too. Rex told her about all the crazy jobs he'd had before starting his own business, funny things he'd seen when he'd been a beer delivery driver, stories from his days in the Marines that he tried to edit so that she'd assume he served in the Philippines during the Spanish-American War, and not in the Middle East in the twenty-first century. She sounded interested, asking more questions and making comments in all the right places, though it was now too dark for him to see her face.

"What brought you here?" she asked.

The answer popped out before Rex could think. "I wanted to see my grandma."

"That's sweet." He could almost hear the smile in Gretchen's voice. "Did you get your visit in before... this?"

"No." He hoped she didn't ask for more details, because he couldn't exactly tell her that it was his great-grandma, and that she was just a little kid right now—if she was even on the island at this exact date and time. He'd figured he'd look for her when he woke from recovery, but hadn't thought past that.

His stomach growled, followed by hers. "Wonder if there's any food in here." Rex was thankful for the diversion.

"If there is, that will be some trick finding it in the dark."

Rex grinned. That problem he could solve. He reached into his pocket for the lighter he always carried, even though he'd quit smoking years ago.

But all he found was his wallet. "What the hell?" He checked the other pocket. Nothing there but his Swiss Army Knife and the keys to his truck. He couldn't see, but felt Gretchen's questioning expression. "Can't find my lighter. Must've dropped it somewhere between here and the water-slide."

He walked to the door and yanked it open, only to be met with a blast of rain and darkness. He slammed the door. "It's no use."

Gretchen stood beside him. "Ah, I probably shouldn't, but..." Her lips smacked, as if she'd pressed them together tight, then opened them quickly. "Perhaps this will help." She pressed something into Rex's hand that felt like a flip-style cell phone.

"What the...?" The metal box flipped open in his palm, and a tiny screen blazed to life.

He'd left his phone in the twenty-first century, he knew that for sure. Besides, his wasn't a flip phone.

He peered at the screen. Instead of the familiar rows of apps, this one looked like a computer menu of sorts, but the stuff on it wasn't like any computer he'd seen.

It was like that thing he'd found in the Dayton Saturn Society House's basement, when he'd gone down there to help Tony out with the water heater in that little back room. Tony had freaked when he saw it in Rex's hand.

Rex flipped the thing shut. "Where the hell did you get this?"

"What is it?" Gretchen asked.

"Where'd you get this?" Rex repeated at the same time.

"Someone gave it to me."

"This is what that guy wanted, isn't it? Why he attacked you," Rex said.

"I... yes. I believe so." Fabric rustled as she sat, as if the admission sapped her strength.

That would explain a lot. The guy's weird clothing that wasn't quite in style, but that she couldn't place. "So why didn't—"

"I- I was told not to give it to anyone—"

"But you gave it to me."

"You didn't let me finish. I was told not to give it to anyone but... you."

Rex drew back. This was getting weirder and weirder. Who from the future knew him? And what the hell was he— would he be—involved in? "Who—" he began again.

"You did. You gave me this strange device. And you told me you would not remember doing so."

"Whoa." Rex's breath escaped in a whoosh as his legs crumpled and he sat beside her. If he'd met her before, it must've been when he'd made a trip further into the past, but from his future...

He shook his head. Just thinking about it was giving him a headache. "So... when did I give this thing to you?"

"You told me not to tell."

Holy Toledo. He must've had a good reason for that. "I'm guessing I told you not to tell me we'd already met either, right?"

"That's correct."

"Huh." Deflated, he rested his head against the building's back wall. The device's screen went dark, just like a smartphone when unused for a couple of minutes.

"I'm sorry," Gretchen said in a timid voice.

"It's okay. I just hope I knew what I was doing." He sighed. "Man, this is some weird shit."

"It certainly is... strange. Do you know what the device does?"

"No. Only that it's really dangerous." Dangerous enough that Tony had visibly shook when Rex had picked up the one in Dayton, and hadn't relaxed until Rex replaced it on the shelf.

Thunder cracked, followed by more rumbling from her belly.

"I wonder if it's at least safe to use it for the light," Rex said.

"It is, as long as you don't touch any of the symbols or words on it."

Rex raised an eyebrow. "How do—"

"You've used it like that before. As a light, I mean."

"Oh. Okay." Feeling his way along the crates, Rex flipped the device open again.

Although it was illuminated from behind like a standard smartphone screen, the display looked like a high-quality printout on nice paper. The background was a dark green, with menu items in white text that didn't sound very phone-like. Select Calendar, read the top one, with the selection shown as Gregorian and the date being September 12, 1916. Other menu items were weird things like Temporalocate, Temporaltrack, Geotrack, and Vitals. (The last three all had a selection of "No Sensor.") One hell of a weird PDA.

"Did you find anything?" Gretchen called.

"Uh, not yet." Better not mess with the smartphone thingy. Rex turned the device away from him, so that its light cast a faint glow on the nearest stack of boxes. More cotton candy sugar, popcorn… "Roasted, salted peanuts?"

"Peanuts would be wonderful."

"One bag of wonderful, coming right up," Rex said in a sing-song voice. He thought he heard faint laughter as he set the strange phone thing on top of a stack of boxes—luckily, it stayed lit—and cut into the box with his Swiss Army knife and pulled out a crimped, paper bag of peanuts in the shell. He laid the bag across his stretched out hand and presented it to her with a flourish. "One bag of our finest, roasted, salted peanuts for the lady." The PDA gave off enough of a glow that he could see her smile. Following the voice in his head to

Put-In-Bay, to 1916, and getting stuck in the so-called storm of the century was all worth it.

He sat beside her, tore open the bag, and grabbed a handful of nuts.

The sound of cracking shells filled the shed, accompanied by the beating rain and the occasional peal of thunder. The smartphone thing turned off after a few minutes, again plunging them into darkness.

They talked about all kinds of things—Rex's life in the military, before he became Rex the Chainsaw Guy, how Gretchen got into the band despite her parents' continual efforts to steer her into a proper marriage by hooking her up with their friends' sons; events in the news (Rex drew on his vague knowledge of history and mostly pretended to know what Gretchen was talking about), and whether or not the water toboggan (as Gretchen called it) would survive the storm. Rex told her about growing up with a dad who gambled for a living—if you could call it that—not knowing when the electric might get shut off again if the Lakers lost, or if they won, which fancy steakhouse they'd go to for dinner.

"What are Lakers?" Gretchen asked.

Oops. "Uh... a professional basketball team." Rex was thankful when she said something comparing his childhood to her own, as he didn't want to have to explain the NBA when he was pretty sure it didn't exist yet.

Gretchen told him about being made fun of all through school because her family was poor—she had a sickly brother whose medical care took priority over nice clothes, and she'd gone to work at age sixteen to provide for herself as much as possible. What made it all bearable was playing baseball in the all-girls' league, and learning to play her grandfather's saxophone, getting lost in the music.

It tugged at Rex's heart, and he couldn't stop himself from scooting closer, his arm almost touching hers.

When she shivered, it seemed the most natural thing in the world to slip his arm around her. Then he realized what he was doing and started to pull away—

"That feels nice," she said, so quietly he could barely hear her over the pounding rain.

"No reason to be colder than we have to be." Of course, Rex could think of even better ways to warm up, but—

Honor. Always that. Besides, Gretchen wasn't a love-'em-and-leave-'em kind of girl. And that was exactly what he'd have to do, whether he wanted to or not.

He rubbed his hand up and down her far arm. "I'm only in town for a couple of days, or I'd ask you out. For when we get out of here, I mean."

She stiffened against him. "Out where?"

Damn, he'd screwed up again. "Uh, out somewhere for fun. A social thing."

"Oh! You mean... like courting?"

"Well, yeah."

"They certainly do have odd ways of saying things in Dayton." She leaned into him more firmly. "I'm afraid Ritchie's committed us to several gigs in Windsor, Ontario, or I should like very much to go out with you."

He pulled her closer against him, ignoring the small, logical side of his brain that told him what a dumb thing to do it was. "I don't know if I could go out with you just once." That was one hundred percent the truth, in more ways than one.

"That's sweet of you." She snuggled into his side. "Maybe we could... pretend. That you didn't have to go back to Dayton. And I didn't have to go on to Ontario."

Whoa, she was coming on to him! "I like that idea." Rex's damned sense of honor crept away, but remained in the background, hovering like a stray cat no one could get to leave.

But it had gone far enough, and when Gretchen shifted against him, he knew she'd lifted her face toward his, and his honorable self kept quiet while he lowered his face and found her lips in a kiss. She moved closer, until her body pressed into his, her breasts against his chest. His arms wrapped around her and he pulled her tightly against him.

When she finally drew away, it was only to breathe.

Rex shifted her onto his lap and held her close. "This sure beats freezing, doesn't it?"

"It's not so bad after all, being trapped in here, with you." She settled into him, her cheek on his chest. Her hair smelled like rain and something sweet and fruity, and Rex wanted to thread his fingers through it. Then he realized nothing was stopping him, and did just that.

They kissed some more. They talked some more. Rex

held her, and it felt fantastic. It had been over a year since he'd had a girlfriend, several since he'd gotten divorced, when his wife had decided she couldn't deal with being alone all the time when he was deployed. He'd forgotten how good it felt to just hold a woman, have someone to talk to, someone who didn't judge or try to tell him what to do, but just listened, and offered an opinion if asked. Who treated him as if he wasn't just a redneck slob, but a hero.

Rex supposed to Gretchen, he was, and that felt good, too.

All the while, the storm raged on outside, and it didn't matter. He and Gretchen had each other, and while peanuts weren't much to live on, they'd do for the time they were stuck there.

Gretchen's chatter had slowed, the silences between her questions stretched out longer and longer. She had to be getting tired; Rex knew he was.

She shifted on his lap and settled her head in the space beneath his shoulder. "I have an aunt and uncle in southern Ohio," she said. "Perhaps I should go visit them when the band breaks for winter."

"Where do they live?"

"They have a farm. My mother says it's quite nice, just outside a small town called Bell.. creek? Something like that—"

"Bellbrook?"

"Yes! That's it."

"That's not far from where I live—" Rex clamped his

mouth shut. Why had he said that?

Gretchen sat upright. "In that case, I shall write to them soon after I return and arrange it. Because I do want to see you again..."

"Uh... I don't know if that's such a good idea."

"Why not?" She tensed. "Oh no, let me guess. You have a girl—"

"No, it's not that."

"Then what? I can't imagine that I'll be touring with the band forever. If Ritchie and Mary don't work out their differences, maybe not even next spring. Who knows what's next for me?"

Rex stared into the darkness. "It's... hard to explain." Tony and Taylor and Violet had been really insistent that he keep the Society, and their abilities, a secret.

"Try me," Gretchen said. "I'll bet I understand more than you think. I'm no simpleton."

"Oh boy." Rex blew out a breath through pursed lips. "It's not that, either. It's... something I'm not supposed to talk about."

"Military secrets?"

"Something like that."

"Oh." She slumped, like a balloon that lost too much air, and it tore at him.

He hated lying to her, even if it wasn't really lying, but more letting her think it was something different than the truth. He hated not telling her what he was, or worse, letting her make a wasted trip, and thinking he'd lied to her.

He spoke slowly. "If you come to Dayton, you'll never find me. Even though I'd totally want you to."

"So why can't you just give me your address?"

"You wouldn't be able to find it."

She straightened. "Oh, I assure you, I'm quite good with maps and directions."

"No, I mean it doesn't exist." Rex sighed. Man, he was getting in deeper with each question.

"You mean... you're a drifter?"

"No, I have a home, just not in this ti..." Damn, he'd said too much.

"In this what?"

Rex clenched his teeth and slowly exhaled. He'd never been good at keeping secrets, and getting this time-travel thing hadn't changed that.

What the hell. "In this time." He slowly rubbed up and down her back, and she relaxed a tiny bit. "I'm... you're going to think I'm crazy."

"Well, in the time we've spent together..." She seemed to choose her words carefully. "You haven't seemed any such thing. Perhaps you should let me be the one to decide what I think."

Rex gave a nod, then remembered she couldn't see him any more than he could see her. "Okay. But if you tell anyone, they'll think you're crazy." And maybe the Saturn Society would come after her. Tony said that happened in some time periods, though Rex didn't know if this was one. "I'm... from the future. The twenty-first century."

"You're from..." She laughed, a nervous giggle. "That sounds like something from a story by the likes of H.G. Wells or Jules Verne."

"I told you you wouldn't believe me—"

"I didn't say that. But... how?"

He told her everything, about his mishap with the chainsaw and waking up in the Saturn Society House to find himself a new member of the organization, whether he wanted to be or not. "My family's come to Put-In-Bay on vacation for generations, starting with my great-great grandparents, about this time," he said. "So... I don't know what, but something made me come up here to try out this time travel thing." He decided to leave out the part about hearing voices in his head. The time travel was crazy enough by itself.

"Perhaps your coming here, when this happened to me... it was meant to be," Gretchen said.

"You could be right," Rex agreed. What with him giving her the strange smartphone-like device, he doubted some anonymous hand of fate had led him to the island.

They talked more about family, life, and what they wanted out of it—Gretchen wasn't sure, and Rex wasn't either, with his newfound ability. In the end, Gretchen decided she believed him, especially when he told her about the smartphones he knew, and voiced his suspicion that the device he'd given her was from his near future.

"You should take it back with you," Gretchen said.

"Yeah, that's probably best," Rex said. "Let's just hope no one else comes after you for it."

The next thing he knew, he woke to sunlight seeping in through the crack around the door, though thunder cracked in the distance.

As he looked around, Gretchen stirred in his arms. They'd fallen asleep on the floor, with her in his protective grasp. "Storm's over," she mumbled.

"Maybe." Rex sat up and listened. Thunder boomed again, closer, only this time it didn't sound quite like thunder, but familiar.

"Is that thunder?" Gretchen said.

"I don't know..." It sounded more like a job site... roof tear-down, that was it. When the workers pulled the old roof off a house, and tossed it into a pile in the yard—

Something slammed against the door, then burst through. "There you are!" A man loomed in the in the bright, morning sunlight.

Rex jumped to his feet, shielding his eyes against the glare. "Who the hell are you—"

"That's him!" Behind him, Gretchen rose. "The man who attacked me!"

The man took a step closer. "Rex Beeber. I might have known. Always a sucker for a damsel in distress. Especially this one."

Rex's lip curled. "Do I know you?" He was sure he'd never seen the guy before. Slimy, used-car-salesman type, with slicked-back hair beneath a detective-style hat and trench coat that made him look like a reject from a 1930s PI movie.

A slow grin spread across the guy's face, increasing the slime factor. "No, but you will." His gaze settled on the stack of boxes where Rex had found the peanuts, and he moved toward them. "I'll just take this—"

"No!" Gretchen leaped for the boxes and snatched the weird PDA-like device from where Rex had left it.

The man lunged for her, but Rex threw himself in his path, and the other man slammed into him. "That belongs to me!"

"It's dangerous!" Gretchen said.

Rex stood firm. "That thing ain't yours. Now get the hell out of here before I show you out through that wall."

"Why, you..." The man tried to push past Rex.

Rex matched his moves, keeping himself between the man and Gretchen. After a couple of minutes, Rex grew bored. "Give it up, man."

The guy stepped backward and gazed at Rex, as if sizing him up. "What are you going to do with it?"

"Take it back to where it belongs."

Before Rex could anticipate the man's move, the guy lowered his head and slammed into Rex's gut, pushing him against the shack's back wall, nearly squashing Gretchen behind him. She sidestepped out of the way with a millisecond to spare, but stumbled, dropping the PDA.

Rex and the other man dove for the device, but the other man was shorter and more nimble, and snatched it from the floor first. He whirled and reached for the door as Rex leaped to his feet and grabbed the guy's collar, yanking him backward. "Not so fast, jackass."

The other man stumbled backward, but didn't drop the device. Rex grabbed both his shoulders and slammed him against the wall. "That ain't yours. Now give it—"

"No!" The guy clutched it to his heart in both hands.

Rex pulled him forward and slammed him into the wall again, rattling the shack. "I can do this all day if you want." The other man was older—probably around forty—and had the belly of a guy who spent a lot more time behind a desk than doing hard, physical work or going to the gym.

Rex slammed the guy again, this time hard enough to make the man's head bang loudly against the wall. The guy clenched his jaw.

Rex repeated the action. The man groaned. "You'll have to..." (slam) "...kill me. And even then..." (slam) "...you won't get it."

"We'll see about that." Rex wasn't even tiring. He slammed the guy's head against the wall one more time with a satisfying crack.

"Rex." Gretchen crept up beside him. "You hold him, and I'll..."

Holding the man pressed to the wall, Rex turned to look at her when the man wrenched free and leaped for the door.

Rex tackled him, and both men crashed to the floor, flinging the futuristic PDA from the man's hands.

As the other man tried to free himself from Rex, Gretchen scrambled for the device. Put her fingers on it.

Dropped it.

It landed inches away from the attacker's hand. Gretchen grabbed for it, and both their hands clutched it at the same time .

Rex leaned up. The other man raised his head. Rex slammed him into the floor, and Gretchen squeezed the device. It flipped open as she pulled it free.

A beam of white light burst from its screen, illuminating the boxes of Health Kups. The carton on top shimmered, then Gretchen snapped the device shut.

The box of cups was gone. "Holy shit!" Rex almost let the man up.

"Wha—" Gretchen began.

"That box of cups just disappeared!"

"Heavens to Betsy!"

The man squirmed beneath Rex. "It's a time control device, you fools. You sent those paper cups to some other time, or maybe even the void."

"What's that?" Rex studied the guy. Had he made a mistake in fighting him?

The man's lips pressed into a line that turned up, as if his knowledge made him superior. "It's a dimension between times, where there is no time. I've been there, and it's enough to drive a man mad—"

"He could have sent us there!" Gretchen held the device at arm's length.

"All the more reason for me to take it back with me."

The man moved beneath Rex, then something sharp

poked the middle of Rex's stomach. "Get off me," the guy grunted. "Or..."

Whatever it was poked harder. Something small and thin, it pricked through the fabric of Rex's shirt—

"Gretchen? Where's my knife?"

The woman drew back, squeezing the futuristic PDA. "I haven't seen it—"

"I have it, you dimwit." The other man shifted beneath Rex. "Now get off of me. This knife may be small, but it won't take much for you to bleed out from the stomach..."

Rex drew back. Damn, the knife must've come out of his pocket when he tackled the guy.

And the guy was right about him bleeding out, too. Slowly, he stood.

The man lurched to his feet, knife pointing at Rex, though his gaze fixed on Gretchen. "Now give me the time control."

"No!"

Then Gretchen did something that Rex never expected. She rushed for him. He reached for her, grasping for the time control device, but instead of handing it to him, she pushed between him and the other man, then burst out the door.

Rex and the attacker hurried after her, just in time to see her pull her arm back and hurl the device as hard as she could toward the waterslide. "Let Lake Erie have the blasted thing!" she shouted as the other man screamed "No!"

Rex stopped on the pier behind her. The other man did the same, almost plowing into him. "I'll dredge the..." the other man began.

But instead of the splash Rex expected, something ka-klunked on the waterslide's staircase.

Rex rushed for the steps, air rushing from his lungs in relief. What would have happened if that thing had gone into the water? Would the water have fried its circuits, or could it have gone off, evaporating the lake into the future?

As Rex crouched to pick it up from the bottom step, the other guy reached him and slammed him against the lattice railing. "Give me..." He grabbed for the device, holding onto Rex's shirt with his other hand, but Rex held the time control out of his reach.

Gretchen came clomping up the pier behind the other man. "Don't give it to him!"

The other guy pushed harder. The lattice creaked under Rex's weight. He glanced down at it. It bowed precariously away from the pier. If he didn't move, the guy would push him into the lake, and would probably get the device—

Rex wrenched aside and bolted up the stairs. He should be able to climb up, scramble down the slide, and get away by the time the other guy reached the top.

Halfway up the rickety staircase, he made the mistake of looking behind him, and realized his other mistake.

He'd underestimated his opponent. The man was only a few paces behind him. And right behind him was something else Rex hadn't counted on: Gretchen.

Another liability.

He couldn't worry about her. Not now. But he could

tell himself that all he wanted, and it wouldn't make a bit of difference—

As Rex set foot on the top platform, the guy grabbed the back of his shirt. "Save us... both the trouble," he said between panted breaths. "If that thing... goes in the... water..."

Rex jerked away from him. "Bite me!" He pulled his hand back to shove the guy down the stairs when Gretchen appeared behind him.

Rex took a step backward.

The other guy kept his gaze focused on Rex, and on the device in Rex's hand. "Why don't you run along, Miss Schwartz? It might be only thirty feet down, but the lake's pretty shallow here, and the bottom's rocky. If you fall, you're liable to hit your head, maybe even die..." Still focused on Rex, he moved forward.

Gretchen held up a hand, and her gaze caught Rex's. She formed a fist with her other hand, and slammed it into her outstretched palm.

Like a baseball.

Rex took another step backward, away from her, and the attacker. He held the device up, took aim, and prayed that her confidence wasn't misplaced—

The other guy rushed him, and Rex threw the time control.

Too slow. Everything happened as if Rex were watching in slow motion.

The other guy jumped for the device. "Noooooo!" Gretchen screamed as she launched herself at the man.

Then everything sped up. No time to see if the guy caught the device before Gretchen slammed into him, knocking him into Rex, who crashed into the single, thin railing. It cracked, buckled, gave way, then Rex was falling... he barely registered the splashes, wetness... and weight as Gretchen fell in the lake on top of him in a tangle of skirts... more weight as the other man landed on top of her. Searing pain burst through Rex's head, and everything went white, then dark.

For the second time in (it seemed) as many days, Rex woke to white.

He managed to pull his arms back enough to push himself up—it felt like someone beat the crap out of him—and looked around.

Hospital ward-like place, but with old-fashioned, brass beds and no medical equipment, the faint buzz of a television down the hall somewhere, and traffic...

Oh yeah, time travel. Some weird, exclusive club called the Saturn Society, which that Taylor chick said he was now part of, whether he wanted to be or not—

No, wait. The bedsheets and the wall beside him were white, but the wall across from him was...

A log house?

Then the rest came back to him. Put-In-Bay, the storm, Gretchen, that weird smartphone that wasn't a phone, and the man who was after it... falling off of that waterslide into the lake, along with Gretchen and that crazy guy.

Rex had banged his head on the rocky bottom pretty bad. Bad enough he might have...

He reached up—damn, was he tired, must be that recovery thing Taylor had told him about—and touched the side of his head. Should be a pretty big gash there, but...

Nothing, not even a spot missing hair—

No, wait, there it was. Not a big gash—well, maybe it was at one time, but now it was a just a scar, a thick line beneath his hair, just over his right ear. Weird.

As if it had happened a hundred years ago.

Rex vaguely remembered being hauled out of the lake, taken to the emergency clinic in Put-In-Bay in a modern-day ambulance, then a guy from the Saturn Society picking him and Gretchen up...

Gretchen! She'd come to the present with him?

His fatigue forgotten, Rex's head whipped around as he sat up the rest of the way.

Like the Saturn Society House in Dayton, the Lake Erie House had a recovery room with four beds in a row. Two glasses and a pewter pitcher sat on the nightstand beside his bed, condensation forming on its sides. In the farthest bed, closest to the log wall, white sheets covered a curvy form, with a cascade of blond hair spilling over the pillow.

All Rex could do was stare. How in the world had she wound up in his time? Brows pressed down, he tried to remember the basics of time travel Taylor had taught him. He must've died when he hit bottom in the lake, and his death brought him back to his own time. The only thing he could figure was that Gretchen had died too, either in the same way, or maybe by drowning, and come by the ability then. And because she'd been holding on to Rex when he'd come back to the present, it had brought her along.

She stirred, as if she'd heard his thoughts. "Gretchen?" he called softly.

Her eyes flipped open, and it was like tiny bits of sky amidst the white and log walls. She opened her mouth, but all that came out was a squeak.

The guy who ran the House had come in and given them drinks of water from a pewter pitcher on the bedside table every now and then. Rex turned around, and there it was, covered in condensation that told him it had recently been filled. He hauled himself to his feet, grabbing the robe off the hook beside his bed and shrugging into it as he stood. "You want some water?"

She made another squeak, which he took as a yes, so he grabbed the pitcher and a glass, and carried them to her.

He filled the glass. "Can you sit up?"

She didn't take her eyes off him. "Mmm-hmm…"

Her shoulders relaxed as he held the glass to her mouth, as if repeating his actions from the Bathing Suit Rentals–Snacks shack put her at ease. Finally, she had enough. "You…" She wiped her mouth on the back of her hand. "Who…? Where am I? What's…?"

Rex's mouth slid open. "You don't remember falling in the lake?" She shook her head. "That weird guy who tried to attack you?" Another shake. "The storm? The Bathing suit rental shed?"

"I'm afraid not."

"Oh boy." Rex blew out a breath. He could only hope that, since they were there and alive in the twenty-first century, that meant the crazy guy hadn't found the time control device.

Yet. In the meantime, Rex had his work cut out for him.

How badly had she hit her head? "You remember me?" Rex asked.

She shook her head. "Not your name, but... I do remember your face." A tiny slip of a smile stole onto her mouth.

"That's a start." Rex reached for her as a grin stretched across his face. "My name's Rex." He took her hand in his, and her eyes held the warmth of the sun. "We'll figure this out, I promise. I've got all the time in the world."

"The Storm" is Episode One of the serialized novel Time's Tempest, *which takes place in a parallel timeframe with* Time's Guardian, *book three of the Saturn Society series by Jennette Marie Powell. Look for "Backlash,"* Time's Tempest *Episode Two, at your favorite online bookseller soon.*

I Wax, I Wane

ANN GREGORY

Like the moon,
moving through its cycle,
I wax, I wane.
Depression follows elation
which follows depression.
Anger follows indifference
which follows anger.
So many thoughts,
so many memories;
so many regrets.
I swell up,
and feel like a real person.
I shrink down,
and know I am insignificant.
I hope, I dream.
I cry, I despair.
I am desolate.
I am invincible.
I am the moon,
moving through its cycle

About the Authors

LINDA CHALK has been writing romances for as long as she can remember. She has completed one historical romance set in the backdrop of the California gold rush. A second one is in progress. She loves to read about American history, especially the old west, and researching all the interesting stuff high school history class left out. Her family often claims that she was born in the wrong century. Writing the family story about *Titanic* was a natural fit.

Judy Carpenter, writing as **ANN GREGORY**, lives in Cherry Grove, a suburb of Cincinnati, Ohio, with her husband Bill and Zacc, a gray and white tom cat. When she's not writing, Judy enjoys painting, sewing, quilting, and traveling with Bill.

DAKOTA JAMES started writing fiction as a young girl when a beloved teacher encouraged her to write ghost stories around Halloween. Dakota quickly switched from writing horror to romantic fiction when she wrote such frightening paranormal stories that she ended up spooking herself. Now, she sleeps better at night writing contemporary romantic stories as opposed to writing about gangsters turning into vampires in a cornfield on the eve of Halloween.

STACY McKITRICK fell in love with paranormal romance, decided to write her own in 2009, and found her passion in life. She used to work in accounting, now she spends her time with vampires, ghosts, and aliens. Born in California, she currently resides in Ohio with her husband. They have two grown children. Look for her debut novel, *My Sunny Vampire*, due out in February 2014 from Lyrical Press, an imprint of Kensington Publishing. Visit Stacy at www.stacymckitrick.com.

SANDY PENNINGTON is an admitted word obsessor. She just can't leave some words or characters alone! Myths, legends and the natural world fuel her imagination. Her favorite thing is curling up with a good book and poring through a dictionary. She gratefully acknowledges her friends and family for the love and inspiration that comes her way.

JENNETTE MARIE POWELL writes time travel and science fiction romance. A life-long resident of Dayton, Ohio, she likes to dig beneath the surface and find the extraordinary beneath the mundane, whether in people, places, or historical events. By day, she wrangles data and websites between excursions to search for the aliens and spacecraft that legends say are stashed away on the military base where she works. Visit Jennette at ww.jenpowell.com.

A Note from the Publisher

Thank you for reading *Love's a Beach*, an anthology of stories of summer love by members of the Ohio Valley Romance Writers of America. Your time is valuable, and this is a privilege the publisher and the authors don't take lightly.

Many thanks to editors Michele Stegman, Lorie Langdon, Barbara Lohr, and Mary Ulrich for their time and expertise and making these stories really shine! We'd also like to thank Jennette Marie Powell for her work on the cover design, formatting the ebook, and designing the print book interior.

If you enjoyed the stories in this book, you may want to check out *Home for the Holidays*, an anthology of holiday stories featuring many of the same authors, available in print and ebook from major online retailers.

Don't miss Stacy McKitrick's debut novel, *My Sunny Vampire*, newly released by Kensington Publishing's Lyrical Press. And, if you enjoyed "Time's Tempest: The Storm" by Jennette Marie Powell, there are several more Saturn Society stories available. *Time's Tempest* Part Two: "Backlash" is slated for release later this year from Mythical Press. Visit Stacy at www.stacymckitrick.com, Jennette at www.jenpowell.com, or stop by www.mythicalpress.com for more information.

— *Publisher, Mythical Press*